Summer

This edition published 2025
by Living Book Press
Copyright © Living Book Press, 2025

ISBN: 978-1-76153-907-7 (hardcover)
         978-1-76153-912-1 (softcover)

First published in 1913.

A catalogue record for this book is available from the National Library of Australia

Summer

by

Dallas Lore Sharp

Contents

1. THE SUMMER AFIELD 5

2. THE WILD ANIMALS AT PLAY 11

3. THE COYOTE OF PELICAN POINT 27

4. FROM T WHARF TO FRANKLIN FIELD 37

5. A CHAPTER OF THINGS TO HEAR THIS SUMMER 43

6. THE SEA-BIRDS' HOME 51

7. THE MOTHER MURRE 58

8. MOTHER CAREY'S CHICKENS 69

9. RIDING THE RIM ROCK 76

10. A CHAPTER OF THINGS TO DO THIS SUMMER 85

11. THE "CONY" 96

A SUMMER EVENING - NIGHT HERONS (page 49)

INTRODUCTION

In this fourth and last volume of these outdoor books I have taken you into the summer fields and, shall I hope? left you there. After all, what better thing could I do? And as I leave you there, let me say one last serious word concerning the purpose of such books as these and the large subject of nature-study in general.

I believe that a child's interest in outdoor life is a kind of hunger, as natural as his interest in bread and butter. He cannot live on bread and butter alone, but he ought not to try to live without them. He cannot be educated on nature-study alone, but he ought not to be educated without it. To learn to obey and reason and feel—these are the triple ends of education, and the greatest of these is to learn to feel. The teacher's word for obedience; the arithmetic for reasoning; and for feeling, for the cultivation of the imagination, for the power to respond quickly and deeply, give the child the out-of-doors.

"If I could teach my Rugby boys but one thing," said Dr. Arnold, "that one thing should be poetry." Why? Because poetry draws out the imagination, quickens and refines and deepens the emotions. The first great source of poetry is Nature. Give the child poetry; and give him the inspiration of the poem, the teacher of the poet—give him Nature. Make a poet of the child, who is already a poet born.

How can so essential, so fundamental a need become a mere

fad of education? A child wants first to eat, then to play, then he wants to know—particularly he wants to know the animals. And he does know an elephant from a kangaroo long before he knows a Lincoln from a Napoleon; just so he wants to go to the woods long before he asks to visit a library.

The study of the ant in the school-yard walk, the leaves on the school-yard trees, the clouds over the school-house roof, the sights, sounds, odors coming in at the school-room windows, these are essential studies for art and letters, to say nothing of life.

And this is the way serious men and women think about it. Captain Scott, dying in the Antarctic snows, wrote in his last letter to his wife: "Make our boy interested in natural history if you can. It is better than games. Keep him in the open air."

I hope that these four volumes may help to interest you in natural history, that they may be the means of taking you into the open air of the fields many times the seasons through.

DALLAS LORE SHARP.

MULLEIN HILL, February, 1914.

SUMMER

CHAPTER I
THE SUMMER AFIELD

The word summer, being interpreted, means vacation; and vacation, being interpreted, means—so many things that I have not space in this book to name them. Yet how can there be a vacation without mountains, or seashore, or the fields, or the forests—days out-of-doors? My ideal vacation would have to be spent in the open; and this book, the larger part of it, is the record of one of my summer vacations—the vacation of the summer of 1912. That was an ideal vacation, and along with my account of it I wish to give you some hints on how to make the most of your summer chance to tramp the fields and woods.

For the real lover of nature is a tramp; not the kind of tramp that walks the railroad-ties and carries his possessions in a tomato-can, but one who follows the cow-paths to the fields, who treads the rabbit-roads in the woods, watching the ways of the wild things that dwell in the tree-tops, and in the deepest burrows under ground.

Do not tell anybody, least of all yourself, that you love the out-of-doors, unless you have your own path to the woods, your own cross-cut to the pond, your own particular huckleberry-patch and fishing-holes and friendships in the fields. The winds, the rain, the stars, the green grass, even the birds and a multitude of other wild folk try to meet you more than halfway, try to seek you out even in the heart of the great city; but the great out-of-doors you must seek, for it is not in books, nor in houses, nor in cities. It is out at the end of the car-line or just beyond the back-yard fence, maybe—far enough away, anyhow, to make it necessary for you to put on your tramping shoes and with your good stout stick go forth.

You must learn to be a good tramper. You thought you learned how to walk soon after you got out of the cradle, and perhaps you did, but most persons only know how to hobble when they get into the unpaved paths of the woods.

With stout, well-fitting shoes, broad in the toe and heel; light, stout clothes that will not catch the briers, good bird-glasses, and a bite of lunch against the noon, swing out on your *legs*; breathe to the bottom of your lungs; balance your body on your hips, not on your collar-bones, and, going leisurely, but not slowly (for crawling is deadly dull), do ten miles up a mountain-side or through the brush; and if at the end you feel like *eating up* ten miles more, then you may know that you can walk, can *tramp*, and are in good shape for the summer.

In your tramping-kit you need: a pocket-knife; some string; a pair of field-glasses; a botany-can or fish-basket on your back; and perhaps a notebook. This is all and more than you need for every tramp. To these things might be added a light camera. It depends upon what you go for. I have been afield all my life and have never owned or used a camera. But there are a good many things that I have never done. A camera may add a world of interest to your summer, so if you find use for a camera, don't fail to make one a part of your tramping outfit.

After all, what you carry on your back or on your feet or in your hands does not matter half so much as what you carry in your head and heart—your eye, and spirit, and purpose. For instance, when you go into the fields have some purpose in your going besides the indefinite desire to get out-of-doors.

If you long for the wide sky and the wide winds and the wide slopes of green, then that is a real and a definite desire. You want to get out, OUT, OUT, because you have been shut *in*. Very good; for you will get what you wish, what you go out to get. The point is this: always go out for something. Never yawn and slouch out to the woods as you might to the corner grocery store, because you don't know how else to kill time.

Go with some purpose; because you wish to visit some particular spot, see some bird, find some flower, catch some—fish! Anything that takes you into the open is good—ploughing, hoeing, chopping, fishing, berrying, botanizing, tramping. The aimless person anywhere is a failure, and he is sure to get lost in the woods!

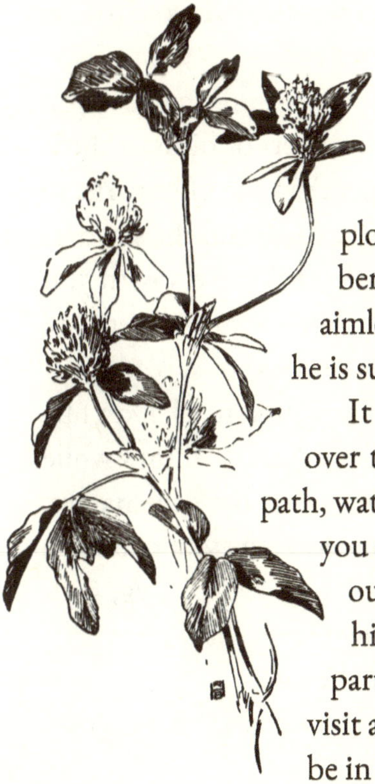

It is a good plan to go frequently over the same fields, taking the beaten path, watching for the familiar things, until you come to know your haunt as thoroughly as the fox or the rabbit knows his. Don't be afraid of using up a particular spot. The more often you visit a place the richer you will find it to be in interest for you.

Now, do not limit your interest and curiosity to any one kind of life or to any set of things out-of-doors. Do not let your likes or your prejudices interfere with your seeing the whole out-of-doors with all its manifold life, for it is all interrelated, all related to you, all of interest and meaning. The clover blossom and the bumblebee that carries the fertilizing pollen are related; the bumblebee and the mouse that eats up its grubs are related; and every one knows that mice and cats are related; thus the clover, the bumblebee, the mouse, the cat, and, finally, the farmer, are all so interrelated that if the farmer keeps a cat, the cat will catch the mice, the mice cannot eat the young bumblebees, the bumblebees can fertilize the clover, and the clover can make seed. So if the farmer wants clover seed to sow down a new field with, he must keep a cat.

I think it is well for you to have some one thing in which you are particularly interested. It may be flowers or birds or shells or minerals. But as the whole is greater than any of its parts, so a love and knowledge of nature, of the earth and the sky over your head and under your feet, with all that lives with you there, is more than a knowledge of its birds or trees or reptiles.

But be on your guard against the purpose to spread yourselves over too much. Don't be thin and superficial. Don't be satisfied with learning the long Latin names of things while never watching the ways of the things that have the names. As they sat on the porch, so the story goes, the school trustee called attention to a familiar little orange-colored bug, with black spots on his back, that was crawling on the floor.

"I s'pose you know what that is?" he said.

"Yes," replied the applicant, with conviction; "that is a *Coccinella septempunctata*."

"Young man," was the rejoinder, "a feller as don't know a ladybug when he sees it can't get my vote for teacher in this deestrict."

The "trustee" was right; for what is the use of knowing that the little ladybug is *Coc-ci-nel'-la sep-tem-punc-ta'-ta* when you do not know that she is a ladybug, and that you ought to say to her:—

> "Ladybug, ladybug, fly away home;
> Your house is on fire, your children alone"?

Let us say, now, that you are spending your vacation in the edge of the country within twenty miles of a great city such as Boston. That might bring you out at Hingham, where I am spending mine. In such an ordinary place (if any place *is* ordinary,) what might you expect to see and watch during the summer?

Sixty species of birds, to begin with! They will keep you busy all summer. The wild animals, beasts, that you will find depend so very much upon your locality—woods, waters, rocks, etc.—that it is hard to say how many they will be. Here in my woods you might come upon three or four species of mice, three species of squirrels, the mink, the muskrat, the weasel, the mole, the shrew, the fox, the skunk, the rabbit, and even a wild deer. Of reptiles and amphibians you would see several more species than of fur-bearing animals,—six snakes, four common turtles, two salamanders, frogs, toads, newts,—a wonderfully interesting group, with a real live rattler among them if you should go over to the Blue Hills, fifteen miles away.

You will go many times into the fields before you can make of the reptiles your friends and neighbors. But by and by you will watch them and note their ways with as much interest as you watch the other wild folk about you. It is a pretty shallow lover of nature who jumps upon a little snake with both feet, or who shivers when a little salamander drops out of the leaf-mould at his feet.

And what shall I say of the fishes? There are a dozen of them in the stream and ponds within the compass of my haunt. They are a fascinating family, and one very little

RED SALAMANDERS, OLD AND YOUNG

watched by the ordinary tramper. But *you* are not ordinary. Quiet and patience and much putting together of scraps of observations will be necessary if you are to get at the whole story of any fish's life. The story will be worth it, however.

No, I shall not even try to *number* the insects—the butterflies, beetles, moths, wasps, bees, bugs, ticks, mites, and such small

NEWTS

"deer" as you will find in the round of your summer's tramp. Nor shall I try to name the flowers and trees, the ferns and mosses. It is with the common things that you ought now to become familiar, and one summer is all too short for the things you ought to see and hear and do in your vacation out-of-doors.

CHAPTER II
THE WILD ANIMALS AT PLAY

The watcher of wild animals never gets used to the sight of their mirthless sport. In all other respects animal play is entirely human.

A great deal of human play is serious—desperately serious on the football-field, and at the card-table, as when a lonely player is trying to kill time with solitaire.

I have watched a great ungainly hippopotamus for hours trying to do the same solemn thing by cuffing a croquet-ball back and forth from one end of his cage to the other. His keepers told me that without the plaything the poor caged giant would fret and worry himself to death. It was his game of solitaire.

In all their games of rivalry the animals are serious as humans, and, forgetting the fun, often fall to fighting—a sad case, indeed. But brutes are brutes. We cannot expect anything better of the animals. Only this morning the whole flock of chickens in the hen-yard started suddenly on the wild flap to see which would beat to the back fence and wound up on the "line" in a free fight, two of the cockerels tearing the feathers from each other in a desperate set-to.

You have seen puppies fall out in the same human fashion, and kittens also, and older folk as well. I have seen a game of wood-tag among friendly gray squirrels come to a finish in a fight. As the crows pass over during the winter afternoon, you will notice their play—racing each other through the air, diving, swooping, cawing in their fun, when suddenly some one's temper snaps, and there is a mix-up in the air.

They can get angry, but they cannot laugh. I once saw what I thought was a twinkle of merriment, however, in an elephant's eye. It was at the circus several years ago. The keeper had just set down for one of the elephants a bucket of water which a perspiring youth had brought in. The big beast sucked it quietly up,—the whole of it,—swung gently around as if to thank the perspiring boy, then soused him, the whole bucket-ful! Everybody roared, and one of the other elephants joined in with trumpetings, so huge and jolly was the joke.

The elephant who played the trick looked solemn enough, except for a twitch at the lips and a glint in the eye. There is something of a smile about every elephant's lips, to be sure, and fun is so contagious that one should hesitate to say that he saw an elephant laugh. But if that elephant didn't laugh, it was not his fault.

From the elephant to the infusorian, the microscopic animal of a single cell known as the paramœcium, is a far cry—to the extreme opposite end of the animal kingdom, worlds apart. Yet I have seen *Paramœcium caudatum* at play in a drop of water under a compound microscope, as I have seen elephants at play in their big bath-tub at the zoölogical gardens.

Place a drop of stagnant water under your microscope and watch these atoms of life for yourself. Invisible to the naked eye, they are easily followed on the slide as they skate and whirl and chase one another to the boundaries of their playground and back again, first one of them "it," then another. They stop to eat, they slow up to divide their single-celled bodies into two cells, the two cells now two living creatures where a moment before they were but one, both of them swimming off immediately to feed and multiply and play.

Play seems to be as natural and as necessary to the wild animals as it is to human beings. Like us the animals play hardest while young, but as some human children never outgrow their youth and love of play, so there are old animals that never grow too fat nor too stiff nor too stupid to play.

The condition of the body has a great deal to do with the state of the spirit. The sleek, lithe otter could not possibly grow fat. He keeps in trim because he cannot help it, perhaps, but however that may be, he is a very boy for play, and even goes so far as to build himself a slide or chute for the fun of diving down it into the water. A writer in one of the magazines tells of an otter in the New York Zoölogical Park that swam and dived with a round stone balanced on his head.

Building a slide is more than we children used to do, for we had ready-made for us grandfather's two big slanting cellar-doors, down which we slid and slid and slid till the wood was scoured white and slippery with the sliding. The otter loves to slide. Up he climbs on the bank, then down he goes—splash—into the stream. Up he climbs and down he goes—time after time, day after day. There is nothing like a slide, unless it is a cellar-door.

How much of a necessity to the otter is his play, one would like to know—what he would give up for it, and how he would do deprived of it. In the case of Pups, my neighbor's beautiful young collie, play seems more needful than food. There are no children, no one, to play with him there, so that the sight of my small boys sets him almost frantic.

His efforts to induce a hen or a rooster to play with him are pathetic. The hen cannot understand. She hasn't a particle of play in her anyhow, but Pups cannot get that through his head. He runs rapidly around her, drops on all fours flat, swings his tail, cocks his ears, looks appealingly and barks a few little cackle-barks, as nearly hen-like as he can bark them, then dashes off and whirls back—while the hen picks up another bug. She never sees Pups. The old white coon cat is better; but she is usually up the miff-tree. Pups steps on her, knocks her over, or otherwise offends, especially when he tags her out into the fields and spoils her hunting. The Society for the Prevention of Cruelty to Animals ought to send some child or puppy out to play with Pups of a Saturday.

I doubt if among the lower forms of animals play holds any such prominent place as with the dog and the keen-witted, intelligent otter. To catch these lower animals at play is a rare experience. One of our naturalists describes the game of "follow my leader," as he watched it played by a school of minnows—a most unusual record, but not at all hard to believe, for I saw recently, from the bridge in the Boston Public Garden, a school of goldfish playing at something very much like it.

This naturalist was lying stretched out upon an old bridge, watching the minnows through a large crack between the planks, when he saw one leap out of the water over a small twig floating

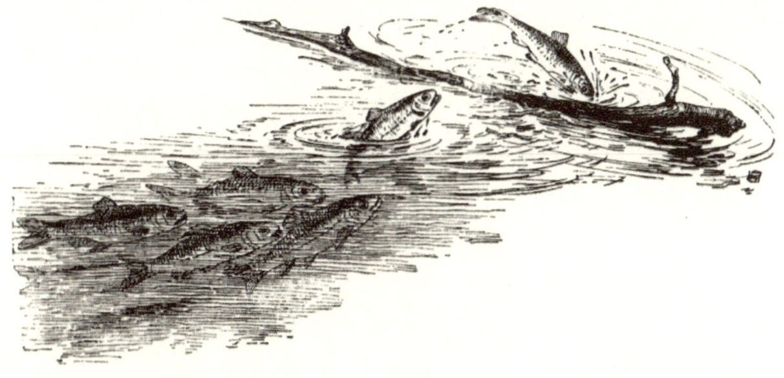

at the surface. Instantly another minnow broke the water and flipped over the twig, followed by another and another, the whole school, as so many sheep, or so many children, following the leader over the twig.

The love of play seems to be one of the elemental needs of all life above the plants, and the games of us human children seem to have been played before the dry land was, when there were only water babies in the world, for certainly the fish never learned "follow my leader" from us. Nor did my young bees learn from us their game of "prisoners' base" which they play almost every summer noontime in front of the hives. And what is the game the flies play about the cord of the drop-light in the centre of the kitchen ceiling?

One of the most interesting animal games that I ever saw was played by a flock of butterflies on the very top of Mount Hood, whose pointed snow-piled peak looks down from the clouds over the whole vast State of Oregon.

Mount Hood is an ancient volcano, eleven thousand two hundred twenty-five feet high. Some seven thousand feet or more up, we came to "Tie-up Rock"—the place on the climb where the glacier snows lay before us and we were tied up to one another and all of us fastened by rope to the guide.

From this point to the peak, it was sheer deep snow. For the last eighteen hundred feet we clung to a rope that was anchored on the edge of the crater at the summit, and cut our steps as we climbed.

Once we had gained the peak, we lay down behind a pile of sulphurous rock, out of the way of the cutting wind, and watched the steam float up from the crater, with the widest world in view that I ever turned my eyes upon.

The draft pulled hard about the openings among the rock-piles, but hardest up a flue, or chimney, that was left in the edge of the crater-rim where parts of the rock had fallen away.

As we lay at the side of this flue, we soon discovered that butterflies were hovering about us; no, not hovering, but flying swiftly up between the rocks from somewhere down the flue. I could scarcely believe my eyes. What could any living thing be doing here?—and of all things, butterflies? This was three or four thousand feet above the last vestige of vegetation, a mere point of volcanic rock (the jagged edge-piece of an old crater) wrapped in eternal ice and snow, with sulphurous gases pouring over it, and across it blowing a wind that would freeze as soon as the sun was out of the sky.

But here were real butterflies. I caught two or three of them and found them to be vanessas (*Vanessa californica*), a close relative of our mourning-cloak butterfly. They were all of one species, apparently, but what were they doing here?

Scrambling to the top of the piece of rock behind which I had been resting, I saw that the peak was alive with butterflies, and that they were flying—over my head, out down over the crater, and out of sight behind the peak, whence they reappeared, whirling up the flue past me on the wings of the draft that pulled hard through it, to sail down over the crater again, and again to be caught by the draft and pulled up the flue, to their evident delight, up and out over the peak, where they could again take wings, as boys take their sleds, and so down again for the fierce upward draft that bore them whirling over Mount Hood's pointed peak.

Here they were, thousands of feet above the snow-line, where there was no sign of vegetation, where the heavy vapors made the air to smell, where the very next day a wild snowstorm wrapped its frozen folds about the peak—here they were, butterflies, playing, a host of them, like so many schoolboys on the first coasting snow!

CHAPTER III
A CHAPTER OF THINGS TO SEE THIS SUMMER

I

The dawn, the breaking dawn! I know nothing lovelier, nothing fresher, nothing newer, purer, sweeter than a summer dawn. I am just back from one—from the woods and cornfields wet with dew, the meadows and streams white with mist, and all the world of paths and fences running off into luring spaces of wavering, lifting, beckoning horizons where shrouded forms were moving and hidden voices calling. By noontime the buzz-saw of the cicada will be ripping the dried old stick of this August day into splinters and sawdust. No one could imagine that this midsummer noon at 90° in the shade could have had so Maylike a beginning.

II

I said in "The Spring of the Year" that you should see a farmer ploughing, then a few weeks later the field of sprouting corn. Now in July or August you must see that field in silk and tassel, blade and stalk standing high over your head.

You might catch the same sight of wealth in a cotton-field, if cotton is "king" in your section; or in a vast wheat-field, if wheat is your king; or in a potato-field if you live in Maine—but

no, not in a potato-field. It is all underground in a potato-field.
Nor can cotton in the South, or wheat in the Northwest, give
you quite the *depth* and the ranked and ordered wealth of long,
straight lines of tall corn.

Then to hear a summer rain sweep down upon it and the
summer wind run swiftly through it! You must see a great field
of standing corn.

III

Keep out from under all trees, stand away from all tall poles,
but get somewhere in the open and watch a blue-black thun-
derstorm come up. It is one of the wonders of summer, one
of the shows of the sky, a thing of terrible beauty that I must
confess I cannot look at without dread and a feeling of awe that
rests like a load upon me.

> "All heaven and earth are still—though not in sleep,
> But breathless, as we grow when feeling most;
> And silent, as we stand in thoughts too deep:—
>
> ....
>
> The sky is changed!—and such a change! Oh night,
> And storm, and darkness, ye are wondrous strong,
> Yet lovely in your strength
>
> ....
>
> Far along,
> From peak to peak the rattling crags among,
> Leaps the live thunder! Not from one lone cloud,
> But every mountain now hath found a tongue,
> And Jura answers, through her misty shroud,
> Back to the joyous Alps who call to her aloud."

IV

But there are many smaller, individual things to be seen this summer, and among them, notable for many reasons, is a hummingbird's nest. "When completed it is scarcely larger than an English walnut and is usually saddled on a small horizontal limb of a tree or shrub frequently many feet from the ground. It is composed almost entirely of soft plant fibers, fragments of spiders' webs sometimes being used to hold them in shape. The sides are thickly studded with bits of lichen, and practiced, indeed, is the eye of the man who can distinguish it from a knot on the limb."

This is the smallest of birds' nests and quite as rare and difficult to find as any single thing that you can go out to look for. You will stumble upon one now and then; but not many in a whole lifetime. Let it be a test of your keen eye—this finding of a little hummer's nest with its two white eggs the size of small pea-beans or its two tiny young that are up and off on their marvelous wings within three weeks from the time the eggs are laid!

V

Have you read Mr. William L. Finley's story of the California condor's nest? The hummingbird young is out and gone within three weeks; but the condor young is still in the care of its watchful parents three months after it is hatched. You ought to watch the slow, guarded youth of one of the larger hawks or owls during the summer. Such birds build very early,—before the snow is gone sometimes,—but they are to be seen feeding their young far into the summer. The wide variety in bird-life, both in size and habits, will be made very plain to you if you will watch the nests of two such birds as the hummer and the vulture or the eagle.

VI

This is the season of flowers. But what among them should you especially see? Some time ago one of the school-teachers near me brought in a list of a *dozen* species of wild orchids, gathered out of the meadows, bogs, and woods about the neighborhood. Can you do as well?

Suppose, then, that you try to find as many. They were the pink lady's-slipper; the yellow lady's-slipper; the yellow fringed-orchis (*Habenaria ciliaris*); the ladies'-tresses, two species; the rattlesnake-plantain; arethusa, or Indian pink; calopogon, or grass pink; pogonia, or snake-mouth (*ophioglossoides* and *verticillata*); the ragged fringed-orchis; and the showy or spring orchis. Arethusa and the showy orchis really belong to the spring but the others will be task enough for you, and one that will give

ORCHIDS
1. *Arethusa bulbosa*
2. *Pogonia ophioglossoides*
3. Pink Lady's-Slipper
4. Yellow Lady's-Slipper
5. Showy Orchis

point and purpose to your wanderings afield this summer.

VII

There are a certain number of moths and butterflies that you should see and know also. If one could come to know, say, one hundred and fifty flowers and the moths and butterflies that visit them (for the flower and its insect pollen-carrier are to be thought of and studied together), one would have an excellent speaking acquaintance with the blossoming out-of-doors.

Now, among the butterflies you ought to know the mourning-cloak, or vanessa; the big red-brown milkweed butterfly; the big yellow tiger swallowtail; the small yellow cabbage butterfly; the painted beauty; the red admiral; the common fritillary; the common wood-nymph—but I have named enough for this summer, in spite of the fact that I have not named the green-clouded or Troilus butterfly, and Asterias, the black swallowtail, and the red-spotted purple, and the viceroy.

Among the moths to see are the splendid Promethea, Cecropia, bullseye, Polyphemus, and Luna, to say nothing of the hummingbird moth, and the sphinx, or hawk, moths, especially the large one that feeds as a caterpillar upon the tomato-vines, *Ma-cros'-i-la-quin-que-mac-u-la'-ta.*

VIII

There is a like list of interesting beetles and other insects, that play a large part in even *your* affairs, which you ought to watch during the summer: the honeybee, the big droning golden bumblebee, the large white-faced hornet that builds the paper nests in the bushes and trees, the gall-flies, the ichneumon-flies, the burying beetle, the tumble-bug beetle, the dragon-fly, the caddis-fly—these are only a few of a whole world of insect folk about you, whose habits and life-histories are of utmost importance and of tremendous interest. You will certainly believe it if you will read the Peckhams' book called "Wasps, Social and Solitary," or the beautiful and fascinating insect stories by the great French entomologist Fabre. Get also "Every-day Butterflies," by Scudder; and "Moths and Butterflies," by Miss Dickerson, and "Insect Life," by Kellogg.

IX

You see I cannot stop with this list of the things. That is the trouble with summer—there is too much of it while it lasts, too much variety and abundance of life. One is simply compelled to limit one's self to some particular study, and to pick up mere scraps from other fields.

But, to come back to the larger things of the out-of-doors, you should see the mist some summer morning very early or some summer evening, sheeted and still over a winding stream or pond, especially in the evening when the sun has gone down behind the hill, the flame has faded from the sky, and over the rim of the circling slopes pours the soft, cool twilight, with a breeze as soft and cool, and a spirit that is prayer. For then from out the deep shadows of the wooded shore, out over the pond, a thin white veil will come creeping—the mist, the breath of the sleeping water, the soul of the pond!

X

You should see it rain down little toads this summer—*if you can!* There are persons who claim to have seen it. But I never have. I have stood on Maurice River Bridge, however, and apparently had them pelting down upon my feet as the big drops of the July shower struck the planks—myriads of tiny toads covering the bridge across the river! Did they rain down? No, they had been hiding in the dirt between the planks and hopped out to meet the sweet rain and to soak their little thirsty skins full.

XI

You should see a cowbird's young in a vireo's nest and the efforts of the poor deceived parents to satisfy its insatiable appetite at the expense of their own young ones' lives! Such a sight will set you to thinking.

XII

I shall not tell you what else you should see, for the whole book could be filled with this one chapter, and then you might lose your forest in your trees. The individual tree is good to look at—the mighty wide-limbed hemlock or pine; but so is a whole dark, solemn forest of hemlocks and pines good to look at. Let us come to the out-of-doors with our study of the separate, individual plant or thing; but let us *go on to Nature*, and not stop with the individual thing.

CHAPTER IV
THE COYOTE OF PELICAN POINT

"We have stopped the plumers," said the game-warden, "and we are holding the market-hunters to something like decency; but there's a pot-hunter yonder on Pelican Point that I've got to do up or lose my job."

Pelican Point was the end of a long, narrow peninsula that ran out into the lake, from the opposite shore, twelve miles across from us. We were in the Klamath Lake Reservation in southern Oregon, one of the greatest wild-bird preserves in the world.

Over the point, as we drew near, the big white pelicans were winging, and among them, as our boat came up to the rocks, rose a colony of black cormorants. The peninsula is chiefly of volcanic origin, composed of crumbling rock and lava, and ends in well-stratified cliffs at the point. Patches of scraggly sagebrush grew here and there, and out near the cliffs on the sloping lava sides was a field of golden California poppies.

The gray, dusty ridge in the hot sun, with cliff swallows and cormorants and the great pouched pelicans as inhabitants, seemed the last place that a pot-hunter would frequent. What could a pot-hunter find here? I wondered.

We were pulling the boat up on the sand at a narrow neck

in the peninsula, when the warden touched my arm. "Up there near the sky-line among the sage! What a shot!"

I was some seconds in making out the head and shoulders of a coyote that was watching us from the top of the ridge.

"The rascal knows," went on the warden, "I have no gun; he can smell a gun clear across the lake. I have tried for three years to get that fellow. He's the terror of the whole region, and especially of the Point; if I don't get him soon, he'll clean out the pelican colony.

"Why don't I shoot him? Poison him? Trap him? I have offered fifty dollars for his hide. Why don't I? I'll show you. Now you watch the critter as I lead you up the slope toward him."

We had not taken a dozen steps when I found myself staring hard at the place where the coyote had been, but not at the coyote, for he was gone. He had vanished before my eyes. I had not seen him move, although I had been watching him steadily.

"Queer, isn't it?" said the warden. "It's not his particular dodge, for every old coyote that has been hunted learns to work it; but I never knew one that had it down so fine as this sinner. There's next to nothing here for him to skulk behind. Why, he has given my dog the slip right here on the bare rock! But I'll fix him yet."

I did not have to be persuaded to stay overnight with the warden for the coyote-hunt the next day. The warden, I found, had fallen in with a Mr. Harris, a homesteader, who had been something of a professional coyote-hunter. Harris had just arrived in southern Oregon, and had brought with him his dogs, a long, graceful greyhound, and his fighting mate, a powerful Russian wolfhound; both were crack coyote dogs from down Saskatchewan. He had accepted the warden's offer of fifty dollars for the hide of the coyote of Pelican Point, and was now on his way round the lake.

The outfit appeared late the next day, and consisted of the two dogs, a horse and buckboard, and a big, empty dry-goods box.

I had hunted possums in the gum swamps of the South with a stick and a gunny-sack, but this rig, on the rocky, roadless shores of the lake—a dry-goods box for coyotes!—beat any hunting combination I had ever seen.

We had pitched the tent on the south shore of the point where the peninsula joined the mainland, and were finishing our supper, when not far from us, back on shore, we heard the doleful yowl of the coyote.

We were on our feet in an instant.

"There he is," said the warden, "lonesome for a little play with your dogs, Mr. Harris."

There was still an hour and a half of good light, and Harris untied his dogs. I had never seen the coyote hunted, and was greatly interested. Harris, with his dogs close in hand, led us directly away from where we had heard the coyote bark. Then we stopped and sat down. At my look of inquiry, Harris smiled.

"Oh, no, we're not after coyotes to-night, not *that* coyote, anyhow," he said. "You know a coyote is made up of equal parts of curiosity, cowardice, and craft; and it's a long hunt unless you can get a lead on his curiosity. We are not out for *him*. He sees that. In fact, we'll amble back now—but we'll manage to get up along the crest of that little ridge where he is sitting, so that the dogs can follow him whichever way he runs. You hunt coyotes wholly by sight, you know."

The little trick worked perfectly. The coyote, curious to see what we were doing, had risen to his feet, and stood, plainly outlined against the sky. He was entirely unsuspecting, and as we approached, only edged and backed, more apparently to get a sight of the dogs behind us than through any fear.

Suddenly Harris stepped from before the dogs, pointed them toward the coyote, and slipped their leashes. The hounds were trained to the work. There was just an instant's pause, a quick yelp, then two doubling, reaching forms ahead of us, with a little line of dust between.

The coyote saw them coming, and started to run, not hurriedly, however, for he had had many a run before. He was not afraid, and kept looking behind to see what manner of dog was after him this time.

But he was not long in making up his mind that this was an entirely new kind, for in less than three minutes the hounds had halved the distance that separated him from them. At first, the big wolfhound was in the lead. Then, as if it had taken him till this time to find all four of his long legs, the greyhound pulled himself together, and in a burst of speed that was astonishing, passed his heavier companion.

We raced along the ridge to see the finish. But the coyote ahead of the dogs was no novice. He knew the game perfectly. He saw the gap closing behind him. Had he been young, he would have been seized by fear; would have darted right and left, mouthing and snapping in abject terror. Instead of that, he dug his nails into the shore, and with all his wits about him, sped for the desert. The greyhound was close behind him.

I held my breath. Harris, I think, would have taken his fifty dollars then and there! And the warden would have handed it to him, despite his past experience with the beast; but suddenly the coyote headed straight off for a low manzanita bush that stood up amid the scraggly sagebrush back from the shore.

The hunt was now going directly from us, with the dust and the wolfhound behind, following the line in front. The gap between the greyhound and the coyote seemed to have closed, and when the hound took the low manzanita with a bound that was half-somersault, Harris exclaimed, "He's nailed him!" and we ran ahead to see the wolfhound complete the job.

The wolfhound, however, kept right on across the desert; the greyhound lagged uncertainly far behind; in the lead, ahead of the big grizzled wolfhound, bobbed the form of a fleeing jack-rabbit!

The look of astonishment and then of disgust on Harris's face was amusing to see. The warden may have been disappointed, but he did not take any pains to repress a chuckle.

Harris said nothing. He was searching the stunted sagebrush off to the left of us. We followed his eyes, and he and the warden, both experienced plainsmen, picked out the skulking, shadowy shape of the coyote, as the creature, with belly to the ground, slunk off out of sight.

It was too late for any further attempt that night.

"An old stager, sure," Harris commented, as we returned to camp. "Knows a trick or two for every one of mine. But I'll fix him."

Nothing was seen of the coyote all the early part of the next day, and no effort was made to find him; but toward the middle of the afternoon, Harris hitched up the bronco, and, unpacking a flat package in the bottom of the buckboard, showed us a large glass window, which he fitted as a door into one end of the big dry-goods box. Then into the glass-ended box he put the two hounds.

"Now, gentlemen," he said, "I'm going to invite you to take a sight-seeing trip on this auto out into the sagebrush. Incidentally, if you chance to see a coyote, don't mention it."

If all the coyotes, jack-rabbits, gophers, and pelicans of the territory had come out to see us thump and bump over the dry, uneven desert, I should not have been surprised; and so, on coming back to camp, it was with no wonder at all that I discovered the coyote, out on the point, staring at us from across the neck of the peninsula. Nothing like this had happened on his side of the lake before.

Harris saw him instantly, and was quick to recognize our advantage. We had the coyote cornered—out on the long, narrow peninsula, where the dogs must run him down. The wily creature had so far forgotten himself as to get caught between us and the ridge along shore, and, partly in curiosity, had kept running ahead and stopping to look at us, until now he was past the place where he could skulk back without our seeing him, into the open plain.

Even yet all depended upon our getting so close to him that the dogs could keep him constantly in sight. The crumbling ledges at the end of the point were full of holes and crevices into which the beast could dodge.

We were not close enough, however. With one of us watching the coyote, should he happen to run, Harris turned the bronco slowly round until the glass end of the box in the back of the buckboard was pointing directly at the creature. There was a scramble of feet inside the box. The dogs had sighted the beast. Then Harris started as if to drive away, the coyote watching us all the time.

Instead of driving off, he made a circle, and coming back slowly toward the coyote, gained the top of a little knoll. Had the coyote seen the dogs in the box, he would have vanished instantly; but the box interested and puzzled him.

He stood looking with all his eyes as the procession turned, and once more the glass end of the box was pointed directly toward him. The dogs evidently knew what was expected of them. They were silent, but ready. Suddenly, without stopping the pony, Harris pulled open the glass door, and yelled, "Go!"

And go they did. I never saw hundred-yard runners leap from the mark as those two hounds leaped from that box. The coyote, in his astonishment, actually turned a back handspring and started for the point.

The dogs were hardly two hundred yards behind him, and were making short work of the space between. It seemed hardly fair, and I must say that I felt something like sympathy for the under dog, wild dog though he was; the odds against him were so great.

But the coyote knew his track thoroughly, and was taking advantage of the rough, loose, shelving ground. For the farther out toward the end of the point they ran, the narrower, rockier, and steeper grew the peninsula, the more difficult and danger-ous the footing.

The coyote slanted along the side of the ridge, and took a sloping slab of rock ahead of him with a slow side-step and a climb that brought the dogs close up behind him. They took the rock at a leap, slid halfway across, and scrambling, rolled several yards down the slope—and lost all the gain they had made.

Things began to even up. The chase began to be interesting. Here judgment was called for, as well as speed. The cliff swallows swarmed out of their nests under the overhanging rocks; the black cormorants and great-winged pelicans saw their old enemy coming, and rose, flapping, over the water; the circling gulls dropped low between the runners; their strange clangor and the stranger tropical shapes thick in the air gave the scene a wildness altogether new to me.

On fled the coyote; on bounded the dogs. He would never escape! Nothing without wings could ever do it! Mere feet could never stand such a test! The chances that pursued and pursuers took—the leaps—the landings! The whole slope seemed rolling with stones, started by the feet of the runners.

They were nearing the high, rough rocks of the tip of the point. Between them and the ledges of the point, and reaching from the edge of the water nearly to the top of the ridge, lay the steep golden garden of California poppies, blooming in the dry lava soil that had crumbled and drifted down on the rocky side.

The coyote veered, and dashed down toward the middle of the poppies; the hounds hit the bed two jumps behind. There was a cloud of dust, and in it we saw an avalanche of dogs ploughing a wide furrow through the flowers nearly down to the water. Climbing slowly out near the upper edge of the bed was the coyote, again with a good margin of lead.

But the beast was at the end of the point, and nearing the end of his race. Had we been out of the way, he might have turned and yet given the dogs the slip—for behind us lay the open desert.

Straight toward the rocks he headed, with the hounds laboring up the slope after him. He was running to the very edge of the point, as if he were intending to leap off the cliff to death in the lake below, and I saw Harris's face tighten as his hounds topped the ridge, and senselessly tore on toward the same fearful edge. But the race was not done yet. The coyote hesitated, turned down the ledges on the south slope, and leaping in among the cormorant nests, started back toward us.

He was surer on his feet than were the hounds, but this hesitation on the point had cost him several yards. The hounds would pick him up in the little cove of smooth, hard sand that lay, encircled by rough rocks, just ahead, unless—no, he must cross the cove, he must take the stretch. He was taking it—knowingly, too, and with a burst of power that he had not shown upon the slopes. He was flinging away his last reserve.

The hounds were nearly across; the coyote was within fifty feet of the boulders, when the greyhound, lowering his long, flat head, lunged for the spine of his quarry.

The coyote heard him coming, spun on his fore feet, offering his fangs to those of his foe, and threw himself backward just as the jaws of the wolfhound clashed at him and flecked his throat with foam.

The two great dogs collided and bounded wide apart, startling a jack rabbit that dived between them into a hole among the rocks. The coyote, on his feet in an instant, caught the motion of the rabbit, and like his shadow, leaped into the air after him for the hole.

He was as quick as thought, quicker than either of the

hounds. He sprang high over them,—safely over them, we thought,—when, in mid-air, at the turn of the dive, he twisted, heeled half-over, and landed hard against the side of the hole; and the wolfhound pulled him down.

It was over; but there was something strange, almost unfair, it seemed, about the finish.

Before we got down to the cove both of the dogs had slunk back, cowering from the dead coyote. Then there came to us the buzz of a rattlesnake—a huge, angry reptile that lay coiled in the mouth of the hole. The rabbit had struck and roused the snake. The coyote in his leap had caught the warning whir, but caught it too late to clear both snake and hounds. His twist in the air to clear the snake had cost him his life. So close is the race in the desert world.

CHAPTER V
FROM T WHARF TO FRANKLIN FIELD

Over and over I read the list of saints and martyrs on the wall across the street, thinking dully how men used to suffer for their religion, and how, nowadays, they suffer for their teeth. For I was reclining in a dentist's chair, blinking through the window at the Boston Public Library, seeing nothing, however, nothing but the tiles on the roof, and the names of Luther, Wesley, Wycliffe, graven on the granite wall, while the dentist burred inside of my cranium and bored down to my toes for nerves. So, at least, it seemed.

By and by my gaze wandered blankly off to the square patch of sky in sight above the roof. A black cloud was driving past in the wind away up there. Suddenly a white fleck swept into the cloud, careened, spread two wide wings against it, and rounded a circle. Then another and another, until eight herring gulls were soaring white against the sullen cloud in that little square of sky high over the roofs of Boston.

Was this the heart of a vast city? Could I be in a dentist's chair? There was no doubt about the chair; but how quickly the red-green roof of the Library became the top of some great cliff; the droning noise of traffic in the streets, the wash of waves against the rocks; and yonder on the storm-stained sky those

wheeling wings, how like the winds of the ocean, and the rau-
cous voices, how they seemed to fill all the city with the sweep
and the sound of the sea!

Boston, Baltimore, New York, Philadelphia, Chicago, San
Francisco—do you live in any one of them or in any other city?
If you do, then you have a surprisingly good chance to watch
the ways of wild things and even to come near to the heart of
Nature. Not so good a chance, to be sure, as in the country;
but the city is by no means so lacking in wild life or so shunned
by the face of Nature as we commonly believe.

All great cities are alike, all of them very different, too, in
details; Boston's streets, for instance, being crookeder than
most, but like them all, reaching out for many a mile before
they turn into country roads and lanes with borders of quiet
and wide green fields.

But Boston has the wide waters of the Harbor and the
Charles River Basin. And it also has T Wharf! They did not
throw the tea overboard there, back in Revolutionary days, as
you may be told, but T Wharf is famous, nevertheless, famous
for fish!

Fish? Swordfish and red snappers, scup, shad, squid, squeteague, sharks, skates, smelts, sculpins, sturgeon, scallops, hali-
but, haddock, hake—to say nothing of mackerel, cod, and
countless freak things caught by trawl and seine all the way
from Boston Harbor to the Grand Banks! I have many a time
sat on T Wharf and caught short, flat flounders with my line.
It is almost as good as a trip to the Georges in the "We're Here"
to visit T Wharf; and then to walk slowly up through Quincy
Market. Surely no single walk in the woods will yield a tithe of
the life to be found here, and found only here for us, brought

as the fish and game and fruits have been from the ends of the earth and the depths of the sea.

There is no reason why city children should not know a great deal about animal life, nor why the teachers in city schools should feel that nature study is impossible for them. For, leaving the wharf with its fish and gulls and fleet of schooners, you come up four or five blocks to old King's Chapel Burying-Ground where the Boston sparrows roost. Boston is full of interesting sights, but none more interesting to the bird-lover than this sparrow-roost. The great bird rocks in the Pacific, described in another chapter of this book, are larger, to be sure, yet hardly more clamorous when, in the dusk, the sparrow clans begin to gather; nor hardly wilder than this city roost when the night lengthens, and the quiet creeps down the alleys and along the empty streets, and the sea winds stop on the corners, and the lamps, like low-hung stars, light up the sleeping birds till their shadows waver large upon the stark walls about the old graveyard that break far overhead as rim rock breaks on the desert sky.

Now shift the scene to an early summer morning on Boston Common, two blocks farther up, and on to the Public Garden across Charles Street. There are more wild birds to be seen in the Garden on a May morning than there are here in the woods of Hingham, and the summer still finds some of them about the shrubs and pond. And it is an easy place in which to watch them. One of our bird-students has found over a hundred species in the Garden. Can any one say that the city offers a poor chance for nature-study?

This is the story of every great city park. My friend Professor Herbert E. Walter found nearly one hundred and fifty species of birds in Lincoln Park, Chicago. And have you ever read Mr. Bradford Torrey's delightful essay called "Birds on Boston Common"?

Then there are the squirrels and the trees on the Common; the flowers, bees, butterflies, and even the schools of goldfish, in the pond of the Garden—enough of life, insect-life, plant-life, bird-life, fish-life, for more than a summer of lessons.

Nor is this all. One block beyond the Garden stands the Natural History Museum, crowded with mounted specimens of birds and beasts, reptiles, fishes, and shells beyond number—more than you can study, perhaps. You city folk, instead of having too little, have altogether too much of too many things. But such a museum is always a suggestive place for one who loves the out-of-doors. And the more one knows of nature, the more one gets out of the museum. You can carry there, and often answer, the questions that come to you in your tramps afield, in your visits to the Garden, and in your reading of books. Then add to this the great Agassiz Museum at Harvard University, and the Aquarium at South Boston, and the Zoölogical Gardens at Franklin Park, and the Arnold Arboretum—all of these with their multitude of mounted specimens and their living forms for *you*! For me also; and in from the country I come, very often, to study natural history in the city.

What is true of Boston is true of every city in some degree. The sun and the moon and stars shine upon the city as upon the country, and during my years of city life (I lived in the very heart of Boston) it was my habit to climb to my roof, above the din and glare of the crowded street, and here among the chimney-pots to lie down upon my back, the city far below me, and overhead the blue sky, the Milky Way, the constellations, or the moon, swinging—

"Through the heaven's wide pathless way,
And oft, as if her head she bowed
Stooping through a fleecy cloud."

Here, too, I have watched the gulls that sail over the Harbor, especially in the winter. From this outlook I have seen the winging geese pass over, and heard the faint calls of other migrating flocks, voices that were all the more mysterious for their falling through the muffling hum that rises from the streets and spreads over the wide roof of the city as a soft night wind over the peaked roofs of a forest of firs.

Strangely enough here on the roof I have watched the only nighthawks that I have ever found in Massachusetts. This is surely the last place you would expect to find such wild, spooky, dusk-loving creatures as nighthawks. Yet here, on the tarred and pebbled roofs, here among the whirling, squeaking, smoking chimney-pots, here above the crowded, noisy streets, these birds built their nests,—laid their eggs, rather, for they build no nests,—reared their young, and in the long summer twilight rose and fell through the smoky air, uttering their peevish cries and

ARGIOPE, THE
MEADOW SPIDER

making their ghostly booming sounds with their high-diving, just as if they were out over the darkening swales along some gloomy swamp-edge.

For many weeks I had a big tame spider in the corner of my study there in that city flat, and I have yet to read an account of all the species of spiders to be found dwelling within the walls of any great city. Even Argiope of the meadows is doubtless found in the Fens. Not far away from my flat, down near the North Station, one of my friends on the roof of his flat kept several hives of bees. They fed on the flowers of the Garden, on those in dooryards, and on the honey-yielding lindens which stand here and there throughout the city. Pigeons and sparrows built their nests within sight of my windows; and by going early to the roof I could see the sun rise, and in the evening I could watch it go down behind the hills of Belmont as now I watch it from my lookout here on Mullein Hill.

One is never far from the sky, nor from the earth, nor from the free, wild winds, nor from the wilder night that covers city and sea and forest with its quiet, and fills them all with lurking shadows that never shall be tamed.

CHAPTER VI
A CHAPTER OF THINGS TO HEAR THIS SUMMER

I

The fullness, the flood, of life has come, and, contrary to one's expectations, a marked silence has settled down over the waving fields and the cool deep woods. I am writing these lines in the lamplight, with all the windows and doors open to the dark July night. The summer winds are moving in the trees. A cricket and a few small green grasshoppers are chirping in the grass; but nothing louder is near at hand. And nothing louder is far off, except the cry of the whip-poor-will in the wood road. But him you hear in the spring and autumn as well as in the summer. Ah, listen! My tree-toad in the grapevine over the bulkhead door!

This is a voice you must hear—on cloudy summer days, toward twilight, and well into the evening. Do you know what it is to feel lonely? If you do, I think, then, that you know how the soft, far-off, eerie cry of the tree-toad sounds. He is prophesying rain, the almanac people think, but I think it is only the sound of rain in his voice, summer rain after a long drouth, cooling, reviving, soothing rain, with just a patter of something in it that I cannot describe, something that I used to hear on the shingles

of the garret over the rafters where the bunches of horehound
and catnip and pennyroyal hung.

II

You ought to hear the lively clatter of a mowing-machine.
It is hot out-of-doors; the roads are beginning to look dusty;
the insects are tuning up in the grass, and, like their chorus
all together, and marching round and round the meadow,
moves the mower's whirring blade. I love the sound. Haying
is hard, sweet work. The farmer who does not love his haying
ought to be made to keep a country store and sell kerosene
oil and lumps of dead salt pork out of a barrel. He could not
appreciate a live, friendly pig.

Down the long swath sing the knives, the cogs click above
the square corners, and the big, loud thing sings on again,—the
song of "first-fruits," the first great ingathering of the season,—
a song to touch the heart with joy and sweet solemnity.

III

You ought to hear the Katydids—two of them on the
trees outside your window. They are not saying "Katy did,"
nor singing "Katy did"; they are fiddling "Katy did," "Katy
didn't"—by rasping the fore wings.

Is the sound "Katy" or "Katy did"? or what is said? Count
the notes. Are they at the rate of two hundred per minute?
Watch the instrumentalist—till you make sure it is the male
who is wooing Katy with his persistent guitar. The male has
no long ovipositors.

IV

Another instrumentalist to hear is the big cicada or "harvest-fly." There is no more characteristic sound of all the summer than his big, quick, startling whirr—a minute mowing-machine up on the limb overhead! Not so minute either, for the creature is fully two inches long, with bulging eyes and a click to his wings when he flies that can be heard a hundred feet away! "Dog-days-z-z-z-z-z-z-z" is the song he sings to me.

V

This is the season of small sounds. As a test of the keenness of your ears go out at night into some open glade in the woods or by the side of some pond and listen for the squeaking of the bats flitting and wavering above in the uncertain light over your head. You will need a stirless midsummer dusk; and if you can hear the thin, fine squeak as the creature dives near your head, you may be sure your ears are almost as keen as those of the fox. The sound is not audible to most human ears.

"FLITTING AND WAVERING ABOUT"

VI

Another set of small sounds characteristic of midsummer is the twittering of the flocking swallows in the cornfields and upon the telegraph-wires. This summer I have had long lines of the young birds and their parents from the old barn below the hill strung on the wires from the house across the lawn. Here they preen while some of the old birds hawk for flies, the whole line of them breaking into a soft little twitter each time a newcomer alights among them. One swallow does not make a summer, but your electric light wires sagging with them is the very soul of the summer.

VII

In the deep, still woods you will hear the soft call of the robin—a low, pensive, plaintive note unlike its spring cry or the

THE RED-EYED VIREO

after-shower song. It is as if the voice of the slumberous woods were speaking—without alarm, reproach, or welcome either. It is an invitation to stretch yourself on the deep moss and let the warm shadows of the summer woods steal over you with sleep.

And this, too, is a thing to learn. Doing something, hearing something, seeing something by no means exhausts our whole business with the out-of-doors. To lie down and do nothing, to be able to keep silence and to rest on the great whirling globe is as needful as to know everything going on about us.

VIII

There is one bird-song so characteristic of midsummer that I think every lover of the woods must know it: the oft-repeated, the constant notes of the red-eyed vireo or "preacher." Wilson Flagg says of him: "He takes the part of a deliberative orator who explains his subject in a few words and then makes a pause for his hearers to reflect upon it. We might suppose him to be repeating moderately with a pause between each sentence, 'You see it—you know it—do you hear me?—do you believe it?' All these strains are delivered with a rising inflection at the close, and with a pause, as if waiting for an answer."

IX

A few other bird-notes that are associated with hot days and stirless woods, and that will be worth your hearing are the tree-top song of the scarlet tanager. He is one of the summer sights, a dash of the burning tropics is his brilliant scarlet and jet black, and his song is a loud, hoarse, rhythmical carol that has the flame of his feathers in it and the blaze of the sun. You will know it from the cool, liquid song of the robin both by its peculiar quality and because it is a short song, and soon ended, not of indefinite length like the robin's.

Then the peculiar, coppery, reverberating, or *confined* song of the indigo bunting—as if the bird were singing inside some great kettle.

One more—among a few others—the softly falling, round, small, upward-swinging call of the wood pewee. Is it sad? Yes, sad. But sweeter than sad,—restful, cooling, and inexpressibly gentle. All day long from high above your head and usually quite out of view, the voice—it seems hardly a voice—breaks the long silence of the summer woods.

X

When night comes down with the long twilight there sounds a strange, almost awesome *quawk* in the dusk over the fields. It sends a thrill through me, notwithstanding its nightly occurrence all through July and August. It is the passing of a pair of night herons—the black-crowned, I am sure, although this single pair only fly over. Where the birds are numerous they nest in great colonies.

It is the wild, eerie *quawk* that you should hear, a far-off, mysterious, almost uncanny sound that fills the twilight with a vague, untamed something, no matter how bright and civilized the day may have been.

XI

From the harvest fields comes the sweet whistle of Bob White, the clear, round notes rolling far through the hushed summer noon; in the wood-lot the crows and jays have already begun their cawings and screamings that later on become the dominant notes of the golden autumn. They are not so loud and characteristic now because of the insect orchestra throbbing with a rhythmic beat through the air. So wide, constant, and long-continued is this throbbing note of the insects that by midsummer you almost cease to notice it. But stop and listen—field crickets, katydids, long-horned grasshoppers, snowy tree-crickets: *chwĭ-chwĭ-chwĭ-chwĭ—thrr-r-r-r-r-r —crrri-crrri-crrri-crrri—gru-gru-gru-gru— retreat-retreat-retreat-treat-treat*—like the throbbing of the pulse.

XII

One can do no more than suggest in a short chapter like this; and all that I am doing here is catching for you some of the still, small voices of *my* summer. How unlike those of your summer they may be I can easily imagine, for you are in the Pacific Coast, or off on the vast prairies of Canada, or down in the sunny fields and hill-country of the South.

I have done enough if I have suggested that you stop and listen; for after all it is having ears which hear *not* that causes the trouble. Hear the voices that make your summer vocal—the loud and still voices which alike pass unheeded unless we pause to hear.

As a lesson in listening, go out some quiet evening, and as the shadows slip softly over the surface of the wood-walled pond, listen to the breathing of the fish as they come to the top, and the splash of the muskrats, or the swirl of the pickerel as he ploughs a furrow through the silence.

CHAPTER VII
THE SEA-BIRDS' HOME

After my wandering for years among the quiet lanes and along the winding cow-paths of the home fields, my trip to the wild-bird rocks in the Pacific Ocean, as you can imagine, was a thrilling experience. We chartered a little launch at Tillamook, and, after a fight of hours and hours to cross Tillamook Bar at the mouth of the bay, we got out upon the wide Pacific, and steamed down the coast for Three-Arch Rocks, which soon began to show far ahead of us just off the rocky shore.

I had never been on the Pacific before, nor had I ever before seen the birds that were even now beginning to dot the sea and to sail over and about us as we steamed along. It was all new, so new that the very water of the Pacific looked unlike the familiar water of the Atlantic. And surely the waves were different,— longer, grayer, smoother, with an immensely mightier heave. At least they seemed so, for every time we rose on the swell, it was as if our boat were in the hand of Old Ocean, and his mighty arm were "putting" us, as the athlete "puts" the shot. It was all new and strange and very wild to me, with the wild cries of the sea-birds already beginning to reach us as flocks of the birds passed around and over our heads.

The fog was lifting. The thick, wet drift that had threatened our little launch on Tillamook Bar stood clear of the shouldering sea to the westward, and in over the shore, like an upper sea, hung at the fir-girt middles of the mountains, as level and as gray as the sea below. There was no breeze. The long, smooth swell of the Pacific swung under us and in, until it whitened at the base of the three rocks that rose out of the sea in our course, and that now began to take on form in the foggy distance. Gulls were flying over us, lines of black cormorants and crowds of murres were winging past, but we were still too far away from the looming rocks to see that the gray of their walls was the gray of uncounted colonies of nesting birds, colonies that covered their craggy steeps as, on shore, the green firs clothed the slopes of the Coast Range Mountains up to the hanging fog.

As we ran on nearer, the sound of the surf about the rocks became audible, the birds in the air grew more numerous, their cries now faintly mingling with the sound of the sea. A hole in the side of the middle Rock, a mere fleck of foam it seemed at first, widened rapidly into an arching tunnel through which our boat might run; the swell of the sea began to break over half-sunken ledges; and soon upon us fell the damp shadows of the three great rocks, for now we were looking far up at their sides, where we could see the birds in their guano-gray rookeries, rookery over rookery,—gulls, cormorants, guillemots, puffins, murres,—encrusting the sides from tide-line to pinnacles, as the crowding barnacles encrusted the bases from the tide-line down.

We had not approached without protest, for the birds were coming off to meet us, wheeling and clacking overhead, the nearer we drew, in a constantly thickening cloud of lowering wings and tongues. The clamor was indescribable, the tossing flight enough to make one mad with the motion of wings. The air was filled, thick, with the whirling and the screaming, the

TUFTED PUFFINS

clacking, the honking, close to our ears, and high up in the peaks, and far out over the waves. Never had I been in this world before. Was I on my earth? or had I suddenly wakened up in some old sea world where there was no dry land, no life but this?

We rounded the outer or Shag Rock and headed slowly in opposite the yawning hole of the middle Rock as into some mighty cave, so sheer and shadowy rose the walls above us,—so like to cavern thunder was the throbbing of the surf through the hollow arches, was the flapping and screaming of the birds against the high circling walls, was the deep, menacing grumble of the bellowing sea-lions, as, through the muffle of surf and sea-fowl, herd after herd lumbered headlong into the foam.

It was a strange, wild scene. Hardly a mile from the Oregon coast, but cut off by breaker and bar from the abrupt, uninhabited shore, the three rocks of the Reservation, each pierced with its resounding arch, heaved their huge shoulders from the waves straight up, high, towering, till our little steamer coasted their dripping sides like some puffing pygmy.

Each rock was perhaps as large as a solid city square and as high as the tallest of sky-scrapers; immense, monstrous piles, each of them, and run through by these great caverns or arches, dim, dripping, filled with the noise of the waves and the beat of thousands of wings.

They were of no part or lot with the dry land. Their wave-scooped basins were set with purple starfish and filled with green and pink anemones, and beaded many deep with mussels of amethyst and jet that glittered in the clear beryl waters; and, above the jeweled basins, like fabled beasts of old, lay the sea-lions, uncouth forms, flippered, reversed in shape, with throats like the caves of Æolus, hollow, hoarse, discordant; and higher up, on every jutting bench and shelf, in every weathered rift, over every jog of the ragged cliffs, to their bladed backs and pointed peaks, swarmed the sea-birds, webfooted, amphibious, shaped of the waves, with stormy voices given them by the winds that sweep in from the sea.

As I looked up at the amazing scene, at the mighty rocks and the multitude of winging forms, I seemed to see three swirling piles of life, three cones that rose like volcanoes from the ocean, their sides covered with living lava, their craters clouded with the smoke of wings, while their bases seemed belted by the rumble of a multi-throated thunder. The very air was dank with the smell of strange, strong volcanic gases,—no breath of the land, no odor of herb, no scent of fresh soil; but the raw, rank smells of rookery and den, saline, kelpy, fetid; the stench of fish and bedded guano, and of the reeking pools where the sea-lion herds lay sleeping on the lower rocks in the sun.

A boat's keel was beneath me, but as I stood out on the pointed prow, barely above the water, and found myself thrust forward without will or effort among the crags and caverns, among the shadowy walls, the damps, the smells, the sounds, among the bellowing beasts in the churning waters about me, and into the storm of wings and tongues in the whirling air above me, I passed from the things I had known, and the time and the earth of man, into a monstrous period of the past.

This was the home of the sea-birds. Amid all the din we landed from a yawl and began our climb toward the top of Shag Rock, the outermost of the three. And here we had another and a different sight of the wild life. It covered every crag. I clutched it in my hands; I crushed it under my feet; it was thick in the air about me. My narrow path up the face of the rock was a succession of sea-bird rookeries, of crowded eggs, and huddled young, hairy or naked or wet from the shell. Every time my fingers felt for a crack overhead they touched something warm that rolled or squirmed; every time my feet moved under me, for a hold, they pushed in among top-shaped eggs that turned on the shelf or went over far below; and whenever I hugged the pushing wall I must bear off from a mass of squealing, struggling, shapeless things, just hatched. And down upon me, as rookery after rookery of old birds whirred in fright from their ledges, fell crashing eggs and unfledged young, that the greedy gulls devoured ere they touched the sea.

I was midway in the climb, at a bad turn round a point, edging inch by inch along, my face pressed against the hard face of the rock, my feet and fingers gripping any crack or seam they could feel, when out of the deep space behind me I caught the swash of waves. Instantly a cold hand seemed to clasp me from behind.

I flattened against the rock, my whole body, my very mind clinging desperately for a hold,—a falling fragment of shale, a gust of wind, the wing-stroke of a frightened bird, enough to break the hold and swing me out over the water, washing faint and far below. A long breath, and I was climbing again.

We were on the outer Rock, our only possible ascent tak-

ing us up the sheer south face. With
the exception of an occasional Western gull's and pigeon guillemot's nest,
these steep sides were occupied entirely
by the California murres,—penguin-
shaped birds about the size of a small
wild duck, chocolate-brown above,
with white breasts,—which liter-
ally covered the sides of
the three great rocks
wherever they could
find a hold. If a mil-
lion meant anything,
I should say there were

BRANDT'S CORMORANT

a million murres nesting on this outer Rock; not nesting either,
for the egg is laid upon the bare ledge, as you might place it upon
a mantel,—a single sharp-pointed egg, as large as a turkey's, and
just as many of them on the ledge as there is standing-room
for the birds. The murre broods her very large egg by standing
straight up over it, her short legs, by dint of stretching, allowing her to straddle it, her short tail propping her securely from
behind.

On, up along the narrow back, or blade, of the rock, and over
the peak, were the well-spaced nests of the Brandt's cormorants,
nests the size of an ordinary straw hat, made of sea-grass and
the yellow-flowered sulphur-weed that grew in a dense mat
over the north slope of the top, each nest holding four long,
dirty blue eggs or as many black, shivering young; and in the
low sulphur-weed, all along the roof-like slope of the top, built
the gulls and the tufted puffins; and, with the burrowing puf-

fins, often in the same holes, were found the Kaeding's petrels; while down below them, as up above them,—all around the rock-rim that dropped sheer to the sea,—stood the cormorants, black, silent, statuesque; and everywhere were nests and eggs and young, and everywhere were flying, crying birds—above, about, and far below me, a whirling, whirring vortex of wings that had caught me in its funnel.

CHAPTER VIII
THE MOTHER MURRE

I hear the bawling of my neighbor's cow. Her calf was carried off yesterday, and since then, during the long night, and all day long, her insistent woe has made our hillside melancholy. But I shall not hear her to-night, not from this distance. She will lie down to-night with the others of the herd, and munch her cud. Yet, when the rattling stanchions grow quiet and sleep steals along the stalls, she will turn her ears at every small stirring; she will raise her head to listen and utter a low, tender *moo*. Her full udder hurts; but her cud is sweet. She is only a cow.

Had she been a wild cow, or had she been out with her calf in a wild pasture, the mother-love in her would have lived for six months. Here in the barn she will be forced to forget her calf in a few hours, and by morning her mother-love shall utterly have died.

There is a mother-principle alive in all nature that never dies. This is different from mother-love. The oak tree responds to the mother-principle, and bears acorns. It is a law of life. The mother-love or passion, on the other hand, occurs only among the higher animals. It is very common; and yet, while it is one of the strongest, most interesting, most beautiful of animal traits, it is at the same time the most individual and variable of all animal traits.

This particular cow of my neighbor's that I hear lowing, is an entirely gentle creature ordinarily, but with a calf at her side she will pitch at any one who approaches her. And there is no other cow in the herd that mourns so long after her calf. The mother in her is stronger, more enduring, than in any of the other nineteen cows in the barn. My own cow hardly mourns at all when her calf is taken away. She might be an oak tree losing its acorns, or a crab losing her hatching eggs, so far as any show of love is concerned.

The female crab attaches her eggs to her swimmerets and carries them about with her for their protection as the most devoted of mothers; yet she is no more conscious of them, and feels no more for them, than the frond of a cinnamon fern feels for its spores. She is a mother, without the love of the mother.

In the spider, however, just one step up the animal scale from the crab, you find the mother-love or passion. Crossing a field the other day, I came upon a large female spider of the hunter family, carrying a round white sack of eggs, half the size of a cherry, attached to her spinnerets. Plucking a long stem of grass, I detached the sack of eggs without bursting it. Instantly the mother turned and sprang at the grass-stem, fighting and biting until she got to the sack, which she seized in her strong jaws and made off with as fast as her long, rapid legs would carry her.

I laid the stem across her back and again took the sack away. She came on for it, fighting more fiercely than before. Once more she seized it; once more I forced it from her jaws, while she sprang at the grass-stem and tried to tear it to pieces. She must have been fighting for two minutes when, by a regrettable move on my part, one of her legs was injured. She did not

falter in her fight. On she rushed for the sack as fast as I pulled it away. She would have fought for that sack, I believe, until she had not one of her eight legs to stand on, had I been cruel enough to compel her. It did not come to this, for suddenly the sack burst, and out poured, to my amazement, a myriad of tiny brown spiderlings. Before I could think what to do that mother spider had rushed among them and caused them to swarm upon her, covering her, many deep, even to the outer joints of her long legs. I did not disturb her again, but stood by and watched her slowly move off with her encrusting family to a place of safety.

I had seen these spiders try hard to escape with their egg-sacks before, but had never tested the strength of their purpose. For a time after this experience I made a point of taking the sacks away from every spider I found. Most of them scurried off to seek their own safety; one of them dropped her sack of her own accord; some of them showed reluctance to leave it; some of them a disposition to fight; but none of them the fierce, consuming mother-fire of the one with the hurt leg.

Among the fishes, much higher animal forms than the spiders, we find the mother-love only in the *males*. It is the male stickleback that builds the nest, then goes out and *drives* the female in to lay her eggs, then straightway drives her out to prevent her eating them, then puts himself on guard outside the nest to protect them from other sticklebacks and other enemies, until the young shall hatch and be able to swim away by themselves. Here he stays for a month, without eating or sleeping, so far as we know.

It is the male toadfish that crawls into the nest-hole and takes charge of the numerous family. He may dig the hole, too, as the male stickleback builds the nest. I do not know as to that. But I have raised many a stone in the edge of the tide along the shore of Naushon Island in Buzzard's Bay, to find the under surface covered with round, drop-like, amber eggs, and in the shallow cavity beneath, an old male toadfish, slimy and croaking, and with a countenance ugly enough to turn a prowling eel to stone. The female deposits the eggs, glues them fast with much nicety to the under surface of the rock, as a female might, and finishes her work. Departing at once, she leaves the coming brood to the care of the male, who from this time, without relief or even food in all probability, assumes the rôle and all the responsibilities of mother, and must consequently feel all the mother-love.

Something like this is true of the common hornpout, or catfish, I believe, though I have never seen it recorded, and lack the chance at present of proving my earlier observations. I think it is father catfish that takes charge of the brood, of the swarm of kitten catfish, from the time the spawn is laid.

A curious sharing of mother qualities by male and female is shown in the Surinam toads of South America, where the male, taking the newly deposited eggs, places them upon the back of the female. Here, glued fast by their own adhesive jelly, they are soon surrounded by cells grown of the skin of the back, each cell capped by a lid. In these cells the eggs hatch, and the young go through their metamorphoses, apparently absorbing some nourishment through the skin of their mother. Finally they break through the lids of their cells and hop away. They might as well be toadstools upon a dead stump, so far as motherly care or concern goes, for, aside from allowing the male to spread the eggs upon her back, she is no more a mother to them than the dead stump is to the toadstools. She is host only to the little parasites.

I do not know of any mother-love among the reptiles. The mother-passion, so far as my observation goes, plays no part whatever in the life of reptiles. Whereas, passing on to the birds, the mother-passion becomes by all odds the most interesting thing in bird-life.

And is not the mother-passion among the mammals even more interesting? It is as if the watcher in the woods went out to see the mother animal only. It is her going and coming that we follow; her faring, foraging, and watch-care that let us deepest into the secrets of wild animal life.

On one of the large estates here in Hingham, a few weeks ago, a fox was found to be destroying poultry. The time of the raids, and their boldness, were proof enough that the fox must be a female with young. Poisoned meat was prepared for her, and at once the raids ceased. A few days later one of the work-men of the estate came upon the den of a fox, at the mouth of which lay dead a whole litter of young ones. They had been poisoned. The mother had not eaten the prepared food herself, but had carried it home to her family. They must have died in the burrow, for it was evident from the signs that she had dragged them into the fresh air to revive them, and deposited them gently on the sand by the hole. Then in her perplexity she had brought various tidbits of mouse and bird and rabbit, which she placed at their noses to tempt them to wake up out of their strange sleep and eat. No one knows how long she watched beside the lifeless forms, nor what her emotions were. She must have left the neighborhood soon after, however, for no one has seen her since about the estate.

The bird mother is the bravest, tenderest, most appealing thing one ever comes upon in the fields. It is the rare exception, but we sometimes find the real mother wholly lacking among the birds, as in the case of our notorious cowbird, who sneaks about, watching her chance, when some smaller bird is gone, to drop her egg into its nest. The egg must be laid, the burden of the race has been put upon the bird, but not the precious burden of the child. She lays eggs; but is not a mother.

The same is true of the European cuckoos, but not quite true, in spite of popular belief, of our American cuckoos. For our birds (both species) build rude, elementary nests as a rule, and brood their eggs. Occasionally they may use a robin's or a catbird's nest, in order to save labor. So undeveloped is the mother in the cuckoo that if you touch her eggs she will leave them—abandon her rude nest and eggs as if any excuse were excuse enough for an escape from the cares of motherhood.

How should a bird with so little mother-love ever learn to build a firm-walled, safe, and love-lined nest?

The great California condor is a most faithful and anxious mother; the dumb affection of both parent birds, indeed, for their single offspring is pathetically human. On the other hand, the mother in the turkey buzzard is so evenly balanced against the vulture in her that I have known a brooding bird to be so upset by the sudden approach of a man as to rise from off her eggs and devour them instantly, greedily, and make off on her serenely soaring wings into the clouds.

Such mothers, however, are not the rule. The buzzard, the cuckoo, and the cowbird are the striking exceptions. The flicker will keep on laying eggs as fast as one takes them from the nest-hole, until she has no more eggs to lay. The quail will sometimes desert her nest if even a single egg is so much as touched, but only because she knows that she has been discovered and must start a new nest, hidden in some new place, for safety. She is a wise and devoted mother, keeping her brood with her as a "covey" all winter long.

One of the most striking cases of mother-love which has ever come under my observation, I saw in the summer of 1912 on the bird rookeries of the Three-Arch Rocks Reservation off the coast of Oregon.

We were making our slow way toward the top of the outer rock. Through rookery after rookery of birds we climbed until we reached the edge of the summit. Scrambling over this edge, we found ourselves in the midst of a great colony of nesting murres—hundreds of them—covering this steep rocky part of the top.

As our heads appeared above the rim, many of the colony

took wing and whirred over us out to sea, but most of them sat close, each bird upon its egg or over its chick, loath to leave, and so expose to us the hidden treasure.

The top of the rock was somewhat cone-shaped, and in order to reach the peak and the colonies on the west side we had to make our way through this rookery of the murres. The first step among them, and the whole colony was gone, with a rush of wings and feet that sent several of the top-shaped eggs rolling, and several of the young birds toppling over the cliff to the pounding waves and ledges far below.

We stopped, but the colony, almost to a bird, had bolted, leaving scores of eggs and scores of downy young squealing and running together for shelter, like so many beetles under a lifted board.

But the birds had not every one bolted, for here sat two of the colony among the broken rocks. These two had not been frightened off. That both of them were greatly alarmed, any

one could see from their open beaks, their rolling eyes, their tense bodies on tiptoe for flight. Yet here they sat, their wings out like props, or more like gripping hands, as if they were trying to hold themselves down to the rocks against their wild desire to fly.

And so they were, in truth, for under their extended wings I saw little black feet moving. Those two mother murres were not going to forsake their babies! No, not even for these approaching monsters, such as they had never before seen, clambering over their rocks.

What was different about these two? They had their young ones to protect. Yes, but so had every bird in the great colony its young one, or its egg, to protect, yet all the others had gone. Did these two have more mother-love than the others? And hence, more courage, more intelligence?

We took another step toward them, and one of the two birds sprang into the air, knocking her baby over and over with the stroke of her wing, and coming within an inch of hurling it across the rim to be battered on the ledges below. The other bird raised her wings to follow, then clapped them back over her baby. Fear is the most contagious thing in the world; and that flap of fear by the other bird thrilled her, too, but as she had withstood the stampede of the colony, so she caught herself again and held on.

She was now alone on the bare top of the rock, with ten thousand circling birds screaming to her in the air above, and with two men creeping up to her with a big black camera that clicked ominously. She let the multitude scream, and with threatening beak watched the two men come on. A motherless baby, spying her, ran down the rock squealing for his life.

She spread a wing, put her bill behind him and shoved him quickly in out of sight with her own baby. The man with the camera saw the act, for I heard his machine click, and I heard him say something under his breath that you would hardly expect a mere man and a game-warden to say. But most men have a good deal of the mother in them; and the old bird had acted with such decision, such courage, such swift, compelling instinct, that any man, short of the wildest savage, would have felt his heart quicken at the sight.

"Just how compelling might that mother-instinct be?" I wondered. "Just how much would that mother-love stand?" I had dropped to my knees, and on all fours had crept up within about three feet of the bird. She still had chance for flight. Would she allow me to crawl any nearer? Slowly, very slowly, I stretched forward on my hands, like a measuring-worm, until my body lay flat on the rocks, and my fingers were within three *inches* of her. But her wings were twitching, a wild light danced in her eyes, and her head turned toward the sea.

For a whole minute I did not stir. I was watching—and the wings again began to tighten about the babies, the wild light in the eyes died down, the long, sharp beak turned once more toward me.

Then slowly, very slowly, I raised my hand, touched her feathers with the tip of one finger—with two fingers—with my whole hand, while the loud camera click-clacked, click-clacked hardly four feet away!

It was a thrilling moment. I was not killing anything. I had no long-range rifle in my hands, coming up against the wind toward an unsuspecting creature hundreds of yards away. This was no wounded leopard charging me; no mother-bear defending with her giant might a captured cub. It was only a mother-bird, the size of a wild duck, with swift wings at her command, hiding under those wings her own and another's young, and her own boundless fear!

For the second time in my life I had taken captive with my bare hands a free wild bird. No, I had not taken her captive. She had made herself a captive; she had taken herself in the strong net of her mother-love.

And now her terror seemed quite gone. At the first touch of my hand I think she felt the love restraining it, and without fear or fret she let me reach under her and pull out the babies. But she reached after them with her bill to tuck them back out of sight, and when I did not let them go, she sidled toward me, quacking softly, a language that I perfectly understood, and was quick to respond to. I gave them back, fuzzy and black and white. She got them under her, stood up over them, pushed her wings down hard around them, her stout tail down hard behind them, and together with them pushed in an abandoned egg that was close at hand. Her own baby, some one else's baby, and some one else's forsaken egg! She could cover no more; she had not feathers enough. But she had heart enough; and into her mother's heart she had already tucked every motherless egg and nestling of the thousands of frightened birds, screaming and wheeling in the air high over her head.

CHAPTER IX
MOTHER CAREY'S CHICKENS

"Who has not wondered," I asked, many years ago, "as he has seen the red rim of the sun sink down in the sea, where the little brood of Mother Carey's chickens skimming round the vessel would sleep that night?" Here on the waves, no doubt, but what a bed! You have seen them, or you will see them the first time you cross the ocean, far out of sight of land—a little band of small dark birds, veering, glancing, skimming the heaving sea like swallows, or riding the great waves up and down, from crest to trough, as easily as Bobolink rides the swaying clover billows in the meadow behind the barn.

I have stood at the prow and watched them as the huge steamer ploughed her way into the darkening ocean. Down in the depths beneath me the porpoises were playing,—as if the speeding ship, with its mighty engines, were only another porpoise playing tag with them,—and off on the gray sea ahead, where the circle of night seemed to be closing in, this little flock of stormy petrels, Mother Carey's chickens, rising, falling with the heave and sag of the sea, so far, for such little wings, from the shore!

You will see them, and you will ask yourself, as I asked myself, "Where is their home? Where do they nest?" I hope you will also have a chance to answer the question some time for yourself, as I had a chance to answer it for myself recently, out on the Three-Arch Rocks, in the Pacific, just off the coast of Oregon.

I visited the rocks to see all their multitudinous wild life,— their gulls, cormorants, murres, guillemots, puffins, oyster-catchers, and herds of sea-lions,—but more than any other one thing I wanted to see the petrels, Kaeding's petrels, that nest on the top of Shag Rock, the outermost of the three rocks of the Reservation.

No, not merely to *see* the petrels: what I really wished to do was to stay all night on the storm-swept peak in order to hear the petrels come back to their nests on the rock in the dusk and dark. My friend Finley had done it, years before, on this very rock. On the steep north slope of the top he had found a safe spot between two jutting crags, and, wrapping himself in his blanket as the sun went down behind the hill of the sea, had waited for the winnowing of the small mysterious wings.

Just to sleep in such a bed would be enough. To lie down far up on the ragged peak of this wild sea rock, with the break and swash of the waves coming up from far beneath you, with the wide sea-wind coming in, and the dusk spreading down, and the wild sea-birds murmuring in their strange tongues all about you—it would be enough just to turn one's face to the lonely sky in such a spot and listen. But how much more to hear suddenly, among all these strange sounds, the swift fanning of wings—to feel them close above your face—and to see in the dim dusk wavering shadowy forms, like a troop of longwinged bats, hovering over the slope and chittering in a rapid, unbirdlike talk, as if afraid the very dark might hear them!

That was what I wanted so much to hear and to see. For

down in a little burrow, in the accumulated earth and guano of the top, under each of these hovering shadows, would be another shadow, waiting to hear the beating of the wings and the chitter above; and I wanted to see the mate in the burrow come out and greet the mate that had been all day upon the sea.

This petrel digs itself a little burrow and lays one egg. The burrow might hold both birds at once, but one seldom finds two birds in the burrow together. While one is brooding, the other is off on its wonderful wings—away off in the wake of your ocean steamer, perhaps, miles and miles from shore. But when darkness falls it remembers its nest and speeds home to the rock, taking its place down in the little black burrow, while the mate comes forth and spreads its wings out over the heaving water, not to return, it may be, until the night and the day have passed and twilight falls again.

We landed on a ledge of Shag Rock, driving off a big bull sea-lion who claimed this particular slab of rock as his own. We backed up close to the shelf in a yawl boat, and as the waves rose and fell, watched our chance to leap from the stern of the little boat to the rock. Thus we landed our cameras, food and water, and other things, then we dragged the boat up, so that, a storm arising or anything happening to the small steamer that had brought us, we might still get away to the shore.

It was about the middle of the forenoon. All the morning, as we had steamed along, a thick fog had threatened us; but now the sun broke out, making it possible to use our cameras, and after a hasty lunch we started for the top of the rock—a climb that looked impossible, and that was pretty nearly as impossible as it looked.

It had been a slow, perilous climb; but, once on the summit, where we could move somewhat freely and use the cameras, we hurried from colony to colony to take advantage of the uncertain sunlight, which, indeed, utterly failed us after only an hour's work. But, as I had no camera, I made the best of it, giving all my time to studying the ways of the birds. Besides, I had come to stay on the peak all night; I could do my work well enough in the dark. But I could not do it in the wind and rain.

The sun went into the clouds about four o'clock, but so absorbed was I in watching, and so thick was the air with wings, so clangorous with harsh tongues, that I had not seen the fog moving in, or noticed that the gray wind of the morning had begun to growl about the crags. Looking off to seaward, I now saw that a heavy bank of mist had blurred the sky-line and settled down upon the sea. The wind had freshened; a fine, cold drizzle was beginning to fall, and soon came slanting across the peak. The prospect was grim and forbidding. Then the rain began. The night was going to be dark and stormy, too wet and wild for watching, here where I must hang on with my hands or else slip and go over—down—down to the waves below.

We started to descend at once, while there was still light enough to see by, and before the rocks were made any slipperier by the rain. We did not fear the wind much, for that was from the north, and we must descend by the south face, up which we had come.

I was deeply disappointed. My night with the petrels on the top was out of the question. Yet as I backed over the rim of that peak, and began to pick my way down, it was not disappointment, but fear that I felt. It had been bad enough coming up; but this going down!—with the cold, wet shadow of night encircling you and lying dark on the cold, sullen sea below—this was altogether worse.

The rocks were already wet, and the footing was treacherous. As we worked slowly along, the birds in the gathering gloom seemed to fear us less, flying close about our heads, their harsh cries and winging tumult adding not a little to the peril of the descent. And then the looking down! and then the impossibility at places of even looking down—when one could only hang on with one's hands and feel around in the empty air with one's feet for something to stand on!

I got a third of the way down, perhaps, and then stopped. The men did not laugh at me. They simply looped a rope about me, under my arms, and lowered me over the narrow shelves into the midst of a large murre colony, from which point I got on alone. Then they tied the rope about Dallas, my eleven-year-old son, who was with me on the expedition, and lowered him.

He came bumping serenely down, smoothing all the little murres and feeling of all the warm eggs on the way, as if they might have been so many little kittens, and as if he might have been at home on the kitchen floor, instead of dangling down the face of a cliff two hundred or more feet above the sea.

Some forty feet from the waves was a weathered niche, or

shelf, eight or ten feet wide. Here we stopped for the night. The wind was from the other side of the rock; the overhanging ledge protected us somewhat from above, though the mist swept about the steep walls to us, and the drizzle dripped from overhead. But as I pulled my blanket about me and lay down beside the other men the thought of what the night must be on the summit made the hard, damp rock under me seem the softest and warmest of beds.

But what a place was this to sleep in!—this narrow ledge with a rookery of wild sea-birds just above it, with the den of a wild sea-beast just below it, with the storm-swept sky shut down upon it, and the sea, the crawling, sinister sea, coiling and uncoiling its laving folds about it, as with endless undulations it slipped over the sunken ledges and swam round and round the rock.

What a place was this to sleep! I could not sleep. I was as wakeful as the wild beasts that come forth at night to seek their prey. I must catch a glimpse of Night through her veil of mist, the gray, ghostly Night, as she came down the long, rolling slope of the sea, and I must listen, for my very fingers seemed to have ears, so many were the sounds, and so strange—the talk of the wind on the rock, the sweep of the storm, the lap of the waves, the rumbling mutter of the wakeful caverns, the cry of birds, the hoarse grumbling growl of the sea-lions swimming close below.

The clamor of the birds was at first disturbing. But soon the confusion caused by our descent among them subsided; the large colony of murres close by our heads returned to their rookery; and with the rain and thickening dark there spread everywhere the quiet of a low murmurous quacking. Sleep was settling over the rookeries.

Down in the sea below us rose the head of an old sea-lion, the old lone bull whose den we had invaded. He was coming back to sleep. He rose and sank, blinking dully at the cask we had left on his ledge; then clambered out and hitched slowly up toward his sleeping-place. I counted the scars on his head, and noted the fresh deep gash on his right side. I could hear him blow and breathe.

I drew back from the edge, and, pulling the piece of sail-cloth over me and the small boy at my side, turned my face up to the slanting rain. Two young gulls came out of their hiding in a cranny and nestled against my head, their parents calling gently to them from time to time all night long. In the murre colony overhead there was a constant stir and a soft, low talk, and over all the rock, through all the darkened air there was a silent coming and going of wings—wings—of the stormy petrels, some of them, I felt sure, the swift shadow wings of Mother Carey's chickens that I had so longed to hear come winnowing in from afar on the sea.

The drizzle thickened. And now I heard the breathing of the sleeping men beside me; and under me I felt the narrow shelf of rock dividing the waters from the waters, and then—I, too, must have slept; for utter darkness was upon the face of the deep.

CHAPTER X
RIDING THE RIM ROCK

From P Ranch to Winnemucca is a seventeen-day drive through a desert of rim rock and greasewood and sage, which, under the most favorable of conditions, is beset with difficulty; but which, in the dry season, and with a herd of anything like four thousand, becomes an unbroken hazard. More than anything else on such a drive is feared the wild herd-spirit, the quick black temper of the cattle, that by one sign or another ever threatens to break the spell of the rider's power and sweep the maddened or terrorized herd to destruction. The handling of the herd to keep this spirit sleeping is ofttimes a thrilling experience.

Some time before my visit to P Ranch, in Harney County, southeastern Oregon, in the summer of 1912, the riders had taken out a herd of four thousand steers on what proved to be one of the most difficult drives ever made to Winnemucca, the shipping station in northern Nevada.

For the first two days on the trail the cattle were strange to each other, having been gathered from widely distant grazing-grounds,—from the Double O and the Home ranches,—and were somewhat clannish and restive under the driving. At the beginning of the third day signs of real ugliness appeared.

The hot weather and a shortage of water began to tell on the temper of the herd.

The third day was long and exceedingly hot. The line started forward at dawn and all day long kept moving, with the sun cooking the bitter smell of sage into the air, and with the sixteen thousand hoofs kicking up a still bitterer smother of alkali dust that inflamed eyes and nostrils and coated the very lungs of the cattle. The fierce desert thirst was upon the herd long before it reached the creek where it was to bed for the night. The heat and the dust had made slow work of the driving, and it was already late when they reached the creek—only to find it dry.

This was bad. The men were tired. But, worse, the cattle were thirsty, and Wade, the "boss of the buckaroos," pushed the herd on toward the next rim rock, hoping to get down to the plain below to water before the end of the slow desert twilight. Anything for the night but a dry camp.

They had hardly started on when a whole flank of the herd, as if by prearrangement, suddenly breaking away and dividing about two of the riders, tore off through the brush. The horses were as tired as the men, and before the chase was over the twilight was gray in the sage and it became necessary to halt at once and make camp where they were. They would have to go without water.

The runaways were brought up and the herd closed in till it formed a circle nearly a mile around. This was as close as it could be drawn, for the cattle would not bed—lie down. They wanted water more than they wanted rest. Their eyes were red, their tongues raspy with thirst. The situation was a serious one.

But camp was made. Two of the riders were sent back along the trail to bring up the "drags," while Wade with his other men circled the uneasy cattle, closing them in, quieting them, and doing everything possible to make them bed.

But they were thirsty, and, instead of bedding, the herd began to "growl"—a distant mutter of throats, low, rumbling, ominous, as when faint thunder rolls behind the hills. Every plainsman fears the growl, for it usually is a prelude to the "milling," as it proved to be now, when the whole vast herd began to stir, slowly, singly, and without direction, till at length it moved together, round and round, a great compact circle, the multitude of clicking hoofs, of clashing horns, and chafing sides like the sound of rushing rain across a field of corn.

Nothing could be worse for the cattle. The cooler twilight was falling, but, mingling with it, rose and thickened and spread the choking dust from their feet that soon covered them and shut out all but the dark wall of the herd from sight.

Slowly, evenly swung the wall, round and round without a break. Only one who has watched a milling herd can know its suppressed excitement. To keep that excitement in check was the problem of Wade and his men. And the night had not yet begun.

When the riders had brought in the drags and the chuck-wagon had lumbered up with supper, Wade set the first watch.

Along with the wagon had come the fresh horses—and Peroxide Jim, a supple, powerful, clean-limbed buckskin, that had, I think, as fine and intelligent an animal-face as any I ever saw. And why should he not have been saved fresh for just such a need as this? Are there not superior horses to match superior men—a Peroxide Jim to complement a Wade and so combine a real centaur, noble physical power controlled by noble intelligence? At any rate, the horse understood the situation, and though there was nothing like sentiment about the boss of the P Ranch riders, his faith in Peroxide Jim was complete.

The other night horses were saddled and tied to the wheels of the wagon. It was Wade's custom to take his turn with the second watch; but, shifting his saddle to Peroxide Jim, he rode out with the four of the first watch, who, evenly spaced, were quietly circling the herd.

The night, for this part of the desert, was unusually warm; it was close, silent, and without a sky. The near thick darkness blotted out the stars. There is usually a breeze at night over these highest rim-rock plains that, no matter how hot the day, crowds the cattle together for warmth. To-night not a breath stirred the sage as Wade wound in and out among the bushes, the hot dust stinging his eyes and caking rough on his skin.

Round and round moved the weaving, shifting forms, out of the dark and into the dark, a gray spectral line like a procession of ghosts, or some slow morris of the desert's sheeted dead. But it was not a line, it was a sea of forms; not a procession, but the even surging of a maelstrom of hoofs a mile around.

Wade galloped out on the plain for a breath of air and a look at the sky. A quick cold rain would quiet them; but there was no feel of rain in the darkness, no smell of it in the air. Only the powdery taste of bitter sage.

The desert, where the herd had camped, was one of the highest of a series of tablelands, or benches, that lay as level as a floor, and rimmed by a sheer wall of rock over which it dropped to the bench of sage below. The herd had been headed for a pass, and was now halted within a mile of the rim rock on the east, where there was about three hundred feet of perpendicular fall.

It was the last place an experienced plainsman would have

chosen for a camp; and every time Wade circled the herd and came in between the cattle and the rim, he felt its nearness. The darkness helped to bring it near. The height of his horse brought it near—he seemed to look down from his saddle over it, into its dark depths. The herd in its milling was surely warping slowly in the direction of the precipice. But this was all fancy—the trick of the dark and of nerves, if a plainsman has nerves.

At twelve o'clock the first guard came in and woke the second watch. Wade had been in his saddle since dawn, but this was his regular watch. More than that, his trained ear had timed the milling hoofs. The movement of the herd had quickened.

If now he could keep them going and could prevent their taking any sudden fright! They must not stop until they stopped from utter weariness. Safety lay in their continued motion. So Wade, with the fresh riders, flanked them closely, paced them, and urged them quietly on. They must be kept milling, and they must be kept from fright.

In the taut silence of the starless desert night, with the tension of the cattle at the snapping-point, any quick, unwonted sight or sound would stampede the herd—the sneezing of a horse, the flare of a match, enough to send the whole four thousand headlong—blind, frenzied, tramping—till spent and scattered over the plain.

And so, as he rode, Wade began to sing. The rider ahead of him took up the air and passed it on, until, above the stepping stir of the hoofs, rose the faint voices of the men, and all the herd was bound about by the slow, plaintive measure of some old song. It was not to soothe their savage breasts that the riders sang to the cattle, but to prevent the shock of any loud or sudden noise.

So they sang and rode, and the night wore on to one o'clock, when Wade, coming up on the rim-rock side, felt a cool breeze fan his face, and caught a breath of fresh, moist wind with the taste of water in it.

He checked his horse instantly, listening as the wind swept past him over the cattle. But they must already have smelled it, for they had ceased their milling. The whole herd stood motionless, the indistinct forms nearest him showing, in the dark, their bald faces lifted to drink the sweet wet breath that came over the rim. Then they started again, but faster, and with a rumbling from their hoarse throats that tightened Wade's grip on his reins.

The sound seemed to come out of the earth, a low, rumbling mumble, as deep as the night and as wide as the plain, a thick, inarticulate bellow that stood every rider stiff in his stirrups.

The breeze caught the dust and carried it back from the gray-coated, ghostly shapes, and Wade saw that they were still moving in a circle. If only he could keep them going! He touched his horse to ride on with them, when across the black sky flashed a vivid streak of lightning.

There was a snort from the steers, a quick clap of horns and hoofs from within the herd, a tremor of the plain, a roar, a surging mass—and Wade was riding the flank of a wild stampede. Before him, behind him, beside him, pressing hard upon his horse, galloped the frenzied steers, and beyond them a multitude, borne on, and bearing him on, by the heave of the galloping herd.

Wade was riding for his life. He knew it. His horse knew it.

He was riding to turn the herd, too,—back from the rim,—as the horse also knew. The cattle were after water—water-mad—and would go over the precipice to get it, carrying horse and rider with them.

Wade was the only rider between the herd and the rim. It was black as death. He could see nothing in the sage, could scarcely discern the pounding, panting shadows at his side; but he knew by the swish of the brush and the plunging of the horse that the ground was growing stonier, that they were nearing the rocks.

To outrun the cattle seemed his only chance. If he could come up with the leaders he might yet head them off upon the plain and save the herd. There were cattle still ahead of him,—how many, what part of the herd, he could not tell. But the horse knew. The reins hung on his straight neck, while Wade, yelling and firing into the air, gave him the race to win, to lose.

Suddenly they veered and went high in the air, as a steer plunged headlong into a draw almost beneath his feet. They cleared the narrow ravine, landed on bare rock, and reeled on.

They were riding the rim. Close on their left bore down the flank of the herd, and on their right, under their very feet, was the precipice, so close that they felt its blackness—its three hundred feet of fall.

A piercing, half-human bawl of terror told where a steer had been crowded over. Would the next leap crowd them over too? Then Wade found himself racing neck and neck with a big white steer, which the horse, with marvelous instinct, seemed to pick from a bunch, and to cling to, forcing him gradually ahead, till, cutting him free from the bunch entirely, he bore him off into the sage.

The group coming on behind followed the leader, and after

"NECK AND NECK WITH A BIG WHITE STEER"

them swung others. The tide was turning. Within a short time the whole herd had veered, and, bearing off from the cliffs, was pounding over the open plains.

Whose race was it? It was Peroxide Jim's, according to Wade, for not by word or by touch of hand or knee had he been directed in the run. From the flash of the lightning the horse had taken the bit, had covered an indescribably perilous path at top speed, had outrun the herd and turned it from the edge of the rim rock, without a false step or a shaken nerve.

Bred on the desert, broken in at the round-up, trained to think steer as the rider thinks it, the horse knew, as swiftly, as clearly as his rider, the work before him. But that he kept himself from fright, that none of the wild herd-madness passed into him, is a thing for great wonder. He was as thirsty as any of the herd; he knew his own peril, I believe, as none of the herd had ever known anything, and yet such coolness, courage, wisdom, and power!

Was it training? Superior intelligence? More intimate association with the man on his back, and so a farther remove from the wild thing that domestication does not seem to touch? Or was it all by suggestion, the superior intelligence above him riding, not only the flesh, but the spirit?

Not all suggestion, I believe. Perhaps a herd of horses could not be stampeded so easily as these P Ranch cattle. In this race, however, nothing of the wild herd-spirit touched the horse. Had the cattle been horses, would Peroxide Jim have been able to keep himself outside the stampede and above the spirit of the herd?

CHAPTER XI
A CHAPTER OF THINGS TO DO THIS SUMMER

I

First, select some bird or beast or insect that lives with you in your dooryard or house or near neighborhood, and keep track of his doings all summer long, jotting down in a diary your observations. You might take the white-faced hornet that builds the big paper nests in the trees; or the mud wasp, or the toad under the steps, or the swifts in the chimney, or the swallows in the barn. It hardly matters what you take, for every life is interesting. The object is to learn how to follow up your study, how to watch one life long enough, and under circumstances different enough, to discover its many-sidedness, its fascination and romance. Such careful and prolonged study will surely reveal to you something no one else has seen, too. It will be good training in patience and independence.

II

Along with this study of *one* life, keep a list of all the beasts, birds, insects, flowers, etc., that live—I mean, that build nests or dig holes and rear families—in your dooryard or in this "haunt" that I told you in "The Spring of the Year" (see page 39, Sections III and IV) you ought to pick out as your own field of study. This list will grow all through the summer and from year to year. I have a list of seventy-six wild neighbors (not counting the butterflies and insects) that are sharing my fourteen-acre farm with me. How many and *what* wild things are sharing your dooryard, your park, your favorite haunt or farm with you? Such a list of names, with a blank place left for each where observations can be entered from time to time, would be one of the most useful and interesting journals you could keep.

III

All through June and into July you should have a round of birds' nests that you visit daily, and to which you can take your friends and visitors—that is, if you live in or near the country. One will be in the big unused chimney of the house, perhaps, and that will be the first; then one in the barn, or in a bird-house in the yard; or in the pear-or apple-tree hole; one in the lilac or honeysuckle bushes, and then down into the orchard, out into the meadow, on into the woods and back—taking in twenty to thirty birds' nests with eggs and young! Did you ever do it? Can you do it this summer? Don't you think it would be quite as exciting and interesting as going to the circus? I can do it; and if you come out to Mullein Hill in June or July, any one of my small boys will take you on his "birds' nest round."

IV

You should camp out—even if you have to pitch your tent in the back yard or up on the roof! You should go to sleep on a bed of boughs,—pine, or spruce, or hickory, if possible,—or swing your hammock between the trunks of sweet-smelling forest trees, and turn your face up to the stars! You will never want to sleep in a room with closed windows after that. To see the stars looking down upon you; to see the tree-tops swaying over you; to feel the fresh night wind stealing across your face and breathing into your very soul—yes, you must sleep at least *one* night this summer right out on a bed of boughs; but with a blanket of wool and a piece of sail-cloth or rubber coat over you and under you, and perhaps some mosquito-netting.

V

But you must *not* build a fire in the woods, unless you have a guide or older people with a permit along. Fires are terrible masters, and it is almost as dangerous to build a fire in the woods as to build one in the waste-paper basket in the basement of some large store. Along the seashore or by the margin of a river or lake, if you take every precaution, it might be safe enough; but in the woods, if camping out, make all preparations by clearing a wide space down to the bare ground, then see that it is bare ground and not a boggy, rooty peat-bed beneath, that will take fire and smoulder and burn away down under the surface out of sight, to break through, perhaps, a week after you have gone, and set the whole mountain-side afire. Build your fire on bare, sandy earth; have a shovel and can of water at hand, and put the fire out when you are done with it. It is against the law in most States to set a fire out-of-doors after the 1st of April, without a permit from the fire-warden.

Now, after this caution, you ought to go out some evening by the shore with a small party and roast some green corn in the husk; then, wrapping some potatoes in clay, bake them; if you have fish, wrap them in clay with their scales on, and bake them. The scales will come off beautifully when the clay is cracked off, and leave you the tastiest meal of fish and potatoes and corn you ever ate. Every boy and girl ought to have a little camp-life and ought to have each his share of camp-work to perform this summer.

VI

At the close of some stifling July day you ought to go out into the orchard or woods and watch the evening come on—to notice how the wild life revives, flowers open, birds sing, animals stir, breezes start, leaves whisper, and all the world awakes.

Then follow that up by getting out the next morning before sunrise, say at half-past three o'clock, an hour before the sun bursts over the eastern hills. If you are not a stump or a stone, the sight and the smell—the whole indescribable freshness and wonder of it all—will thrill you. Would you go to the Pyramids or Niagara or the Yellowstone Park? Yes, you would, and you would take a great deal of trouble to see any one of these wonders! Just as great a wonder, just as thrilling an experience, is right outside of your bedroom early any June, July, or August morning! I know boys and girls who *never* saw the sun get up!

VII

You ought to spend some time this summer on a real farm. Boy or girl, you need to feel ploughed ground under your feet; you need the contact with growing things in the ground; you need to handle a hoe, gather the garden vegetables, feed the chickens, feed the pigs, drive the cows to pasture, help stow away the hay—and all the other interesting experiences that make up the simple, elemental, and wonderfully varied day of farm life. A mere visit is not enough. You need to take part in the digging and weeding and planting. The other day I let out my cow after keeping her all winter in the barn. The first thing she did was to kick up her heels and run to a pile of fresh earth about a newly planted tree and fall to eating it—not the tree, but the earth, the raw, rich soil—until her muzzle was muddy halfway to her eyes. You do not need to eat it; but the need to smell it, to see it, to feel it, to work in it, is just as real as the cow's need to eat it.

VIII

You ought to learn how to browse and nibble in the woods. What do I mean? Why, just this: that you ought to learn how to taste the woods as well as to see them. Maurice Thompson, in "Byways and Bird Notes," a book you ought to read (and that is another "ought to do" for this summer), has a chapter called

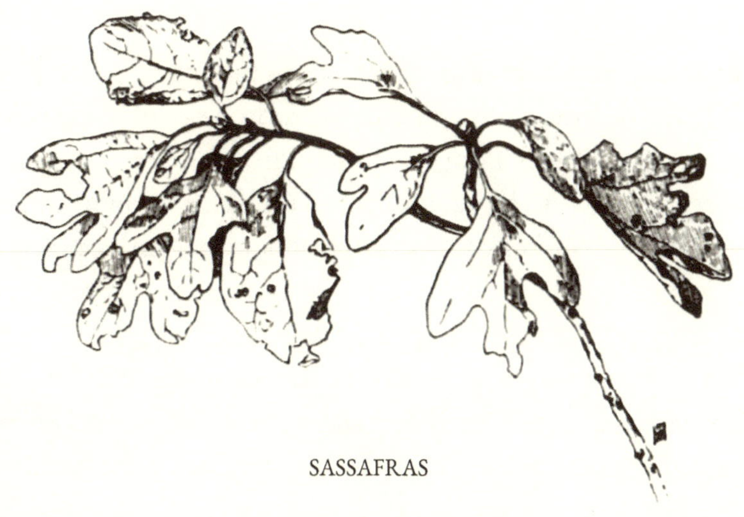

SASSAFRAS

DEADLY NIGHTSHADE

"Browsing and Nibbling" in which his mountain guide says: "What makes me allus a-nibblin' an' a-browsin' of the bushes an' things as I goes along? I kinder b'lieve hit keeps a feller's heart stiddy an' his blood pure for to nibble an' browse kinder like a deer does. You know a deer is allus strong an' active, an' hit is everlastin'ly a-nibblin' an' a-browsin'. Ef hit is good for the annymel, hit otter be good for the feller."

The guide may not be right about the strength to be had from tasting the roots and barks and buds of things, but I know that I am right when I tell you that the very sap of the summer woods will seem to mingle with your blood at the taste of the aromatic sassafras root, the spicy bark of the sweet birch and the biting bulb of the Indian turnip. Many of the perfumes, odors, resins, gums, saps, and nectars of the woods can be known to you only by sense of taste.

IX

"But I shall bite into something poisonous," you say. Yes, you must look out for that, and you must take the pains this

POISON SUMACH

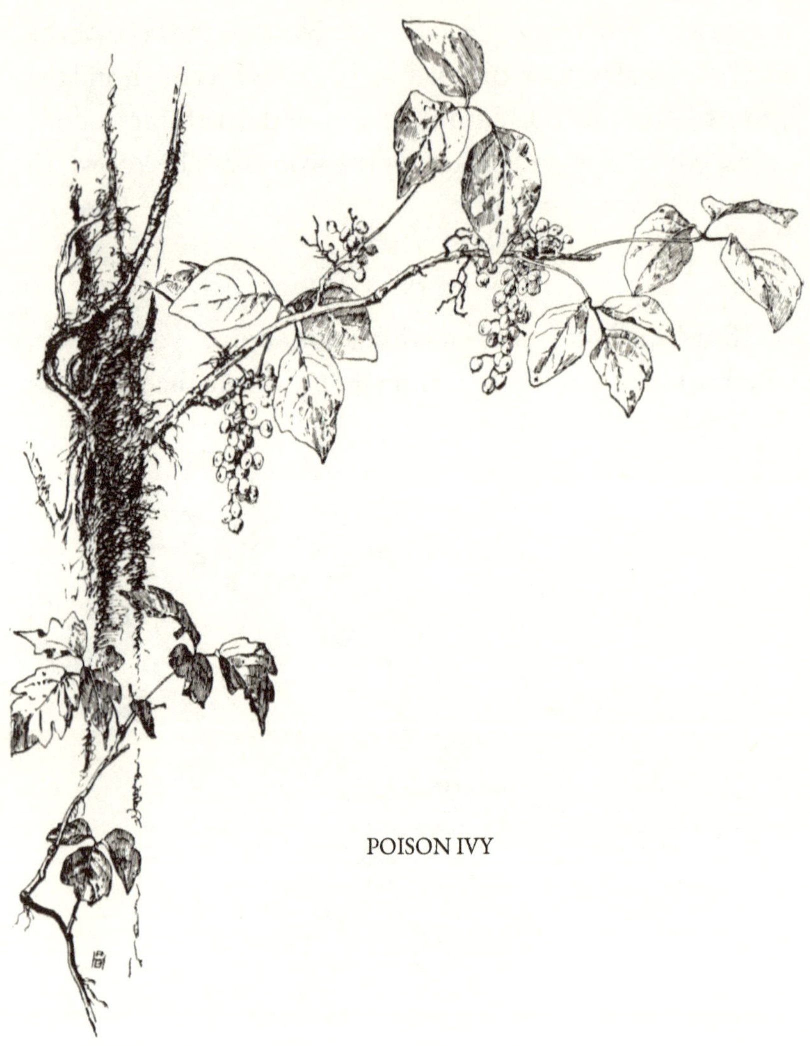

POISON IVY

summer to learn the poisonous things of our woods and fields. So before you begin to browse and nibble, make a business of learning the deadly nightshade with its green or its red berries; the poison sumach with its *loose* panicles or clusters of grayish-white berries; the three-leaved poison ivy or "ground oak" (which you can easily tell from the five-leaved Virginia creeper); and the deadly mushrooms with their *bulbous* roots. These are the poisonous plants that you will meet with most frequently, but there are a few others, and it will be safest not to nibble any plant that is strange to you. Nor am I suggesting that you make a meal on the pitch of the pine trees or anything else. Do not *eat* any of these things; taste them only. I was once made desperately ill by eating poke root (I was a very little child) which I took for sweet potato. Poke berries are not good to *eat*. Take along a few good sandwiches from home to eat. But learn to know the mints, the medicinal roots and barks, and that long list of old-fashioned "herbs" that our grandmothers hung from the garret rafters and made us take occasionally as "tea."

VIRGINIA CREEPER

X

Finally, as a lover of the woods and wild life, you ought to take a personal responsibility for the preservation of the trees and woods in your neighborhood, and of the birds and beasts and other lowlier forms of wild life. Year by year the wild things are vanishing never to return to your woods, and never to be seen again by man. Do what you can to stop the hunting and ignorant killing of every sort. You ought to get and read "Our Vanishing Wild Life," by William T. Hornaday, and then join the growing host of us who, alarmed at the fearful increase of insect pests, and the loss to the beauty and inter-

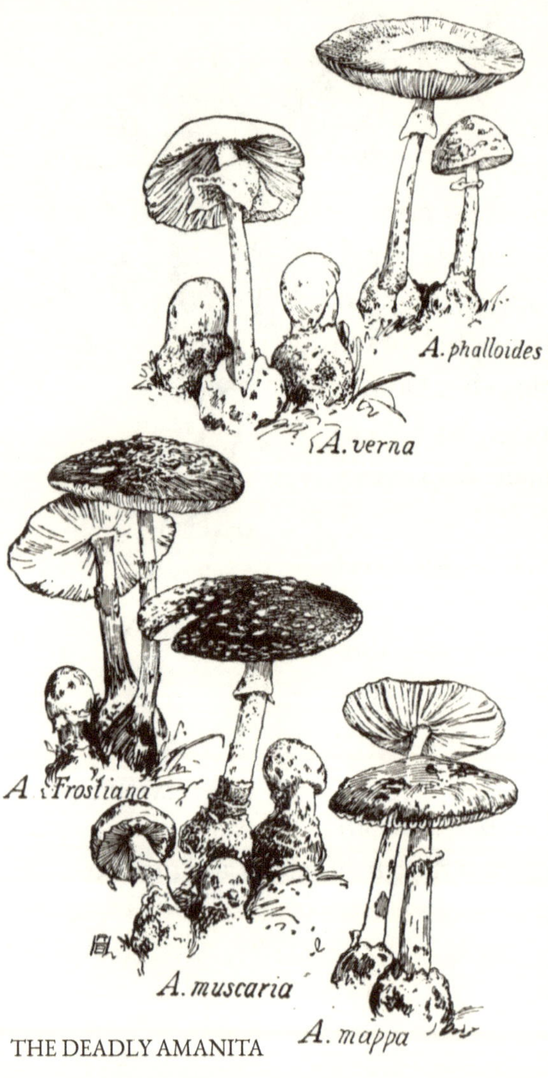

THE DEADLY AMANITA

POKE

est of the out-of-doors through the extermination of wild life, are doing our best to save the wild things we still have and to increase their numbers.

CHAPTER XII
THE "CONY"

We were threading our slow way along the narrow divide of the Wallowa Mountains that runs between the branches of the Snake River. Our guide was a former "camp-tender," one who carries provisions to the sheep-herders in the mountains. As we were stopping a moment to breathe our horses and to look down upon the head springs of Big Sheep and Salt Lick Creeks on one side, and the narrow ribbon of the Imnaha on the other, this guide and our mammal-collector rode on ahead. An hour later I saw them round the breast of a peak far along on the trail and disappear. That night they brought into camp a "cony," or pika, or little chief hare.

The year before, this camp-tender, in passing a certain rock-slide among the high peaks of the pass, had heard and seen a peculiar little animal about the size and shape of a small guinea-pig, whistling among the broken rock. He had never seen the little creature before,—had never heard of it. It was to this slide that he now took our naturalist, in the hope of showing him the mountain guinea-pig, and, sure enough, they brought one back with them, and showed me my first "cony," one of the rarest of American mammals.

But I was broken-hearted. That I should have been so near and missed it! For we had descended to Aneroid Lake to camp that night, and there were no cony slides below us on the trail.

While the men were busy about camp the next morning, I slipped off alone on foot, and, following the trail, got back about ten o'clock to the rock-slide where they had killed the cony.

A wilder, barrener, more desolate land of crags and peaks I never beheld. Eternal silence seemed to wrap it round. The slide was of broken pieces of rock, just as if the bricks from an immense chimney had cracked off and rolled down into the valley of the roof. Stunted vegetation grew around, with scraggly wild grass and a few snow-line flowers, for this was on the snow-line, several melting banks glistening in the morning sun about me.

I crept round the sharp slope of the peak and down to the edge of the rock-slide. "Any living thing in that long heap of broken rock!" I said to myself incredulously. That barren, blasted pile of splintered peaks the home of an animal? Why, I was on the top of the world! A great dark hawk was wheeling over toward Eagle Cap Mountain in the distance; far below me flapped a band of ravens; and down, down, immeasurably far down, glistened the small winding waters of the Imnaha; while all about me were the peaks, lonely, solitary, mighty, terrible! Such bleakness and desolation!

But here, they told me, they had shot the cony. I could not believe it. Why should any animal live away up here on the roof of the world? For several feet each side of the steep, piled-up rock grew spears of thin, wiry grass about six inches high, and a few stunted flowers,—pussy's-paws, alpine phlox, and beardtongue, all of them flat to the sand,—and farther down the sides of the ravine were low, twisted pines,—mere prostrate mats of trees that had crept in narrow ascending tongues, up and up, until they could hang on no longer to the bare alpine slopes. But here above the stunted pines, here in the slide rock, where only mosses and a few flat plants could live,—plants that blossom in the snow,—dwell the conies.

I sat down on the edge of the slide, feeling that I had had my labor for my pains. We had been climbing these peaks in the hope of seeing one of the last small bands of mountain sheep that made these fastnesses their home. But, much as I wished to see a wild mountain sheep among the crags, I wished more to see the little cony among the rocks. "As for the stork," says the Bible, "the fir trees are her house. The high hills are a refuge for the wild goats; and the rocks for the conies." I had always wondered about those conies—what they looked like and how they lived among the rocks.

I knew that these little conies here in the slide (if indeed they *could* be here) were not those of the mountain-peaks of Palestine. What of that! The very rocks might be different in kind from the rocks of Nebo or Lebanon; but peaks are peaks, and rocks are rocks, and the strange little "rabbits" that dwell in their broken slides are all conies to me. The cony of the Bible is the little hyrax, a relative of the elephant.

I sat for a while watching. Was this the place? I must make sure before I settled down to waiting, for when in all my life again might I have this chance?

Out in the middle of the slide was a pile of rocks with an uneven look about them, as if they had been heaped up there by other hands than those that hurled them from the peak. Going quietly out, I examined them closely, and found the perfect print of a little bloody paw on one of them.

This was the right place. Here was where they had shot the specimen brought into camp. I got back to my seat, ready now to wait, even while I knew that I was holding back the camp from its day's march.

Perhaps I had been watching for half an hour, when from somewhere, in the rock-slide surely, though I could not tell, there sounded a shrill bleating whistle, not unlike the whistles of the ground squirrels and marmots that I had heard all through the mountains, yet more tremulous and not so piercing.

I waited. Presently a little gray form crept over a stone, stopped and whistled, then disappeared. It was my cony!

If you can think of Molly Cottontail turned into the shape of a guinea-pig about eight inches long, with positively no tail at all, and with big round broad ears, and with all four legs of equal length so that the creature walks instead of hopping,—if you can imagine such a rabbit,—you will get a pretty clear picture of the cony, or pika, or "little chief hare."

I kept as still as the stones. Presently the plaintive, bleating whistle sounded from nowhere again—behind me, beyond me, up the slide or down, I could not tell. The rocks were rough, rusty chunks two or three feet long, piled helter-skelter without form or order, so that any one spot in the slide looked precisely like every other spot. I could not tell just the piece the cony had crossed, once my eyes were off of it, nor into which of the cracks he had disappeared. I could only sit still and wait till I caught him moving, so completely did his color blend with the rusty brown tone of the slide.

All the while the shrill, piteous call kept coming from anywhere in the slide. But it was not the call of several voices, not a colony whistling at once. The conies live in colonies, but, judging from the single small haycock which they had curing in the sun, I think there could not have been more than two or three pairs of them in this particular slide. Possibly there was only the single pair, one of which had been shot, for presently, when my eyes grew sharp enough to pick the little creature out against the rocks, I found that one was doing all the calling, and that for some reason he was greatly disturbed.

Now he would stop on a slab and whistle, then dive into some long passage under the stones, to reappear several feet or yards away. Here he would pause to listen, and, hearing nothing, would call again, waiting for an answer to his tremulous cry which did not come.

Under and over the stones, up and down the slide, now close to me, now on the extreme opposite edge of the pile he traveled, nervously, anxiously looking for something—for some *one*, I truly think; and my heart smote me when I thought it might be for the dead mate whose little bare foot-pads had left the bloody print upon the rock.

Up and down, in and out, he ran, calling, calling, calling, but getting no answer back. He was the only one that showed himself, the only live one I have ever seen, but this one I followed, as he went searching and crying over the steep rock-slide, with my eye and with the field-glasses, until long past noon—with a whole camp down the cañon looking for me!

But they must know where to look. Let them climb out of the cañon, back to the top of the world to the cony slide, if they could not wait for me.

Higher up than the mountain sheep or the goat can live, where only the burrowing pocket gopher and rare field mice are ever found, dwells the cony. This particular slide was on one of the minor peaks,—loftier ones towered all about,—nor do I know just how high it was, but the cony dwells above the tree-line, up in the Arctic-Alpine Zone, in a world of perpetual snow, from ten to fourteen thousand feet above the sea.

By perpetual snow I mean that the snow-banks never melt in the shadowed ravines and on the bare north slopes. Here, where I was watching, the rock-slide lay open to the sun, the scanty grass was green beyond the gully, and the squat alpine flowers were in bloom, the saxifrage and a solitary aster (April and September together!) blossoming in the edges of the snow just as fast as the melting banks allowed them to lift their heads. But any day the wind might come down from the north, keen and thick and white about the summits, and leave the flowers and the cony slide covered deep beneath a drift.

Spring, summer, and autumn are all one season, all crowded together—a kind of peak piercing for a few short weeks the long, bleak, unbroken land of winter here on the roof of the world.

But during this brief period the thin grass springs up, and the conies cut and cure it, enough of it to last them from the falling of the September snows until the drifts are once more melted and their rock-slide warms in another summer's sun.

For the cony does not hibernate. He stays awake down in his catacombs. Think of being buried alive in pitch-black night with snow twenty-five feet thick above you for nine out of twelve months of the year! Yet here they are away up on the sides of the wildest summits, living their lives, keeping their houses, rearing their children, visiting back and forth through their subways for all this long winter, protected by the drifts which lie so deep that they keep out the cold.

As I looked about me I could not see grass enough to feed a pair of conies for a winter. Right near me was one of their little haycocks, nearly cured and ready for storing in their barns beneath the rocks; but this would not last long. It was already early August and what haying they had to do must be done quickly or winter would catch them hungry.

They cut the grass that grows in the vicinity of the slide, and cock it until it is cured, then they carry it all below against the coming of the cold; and naturalists who have observed them describe with what hurry and excitement the colony falls to taking in the hay when bad weather threatens to spoil it.

Hardy little farmers! Bold small folk! Why climb for a home with your tiny, bare-soled feet above the aerie of the eagle and the cave of the soaring condor of the Sierras? Why not descend to the warm valleys, where winter, indeed, comes, but cannot linger?—or farther down where the grass is always green, with never a need to cut and cure a winter's hay?

I do not know why—nor why upon the tossing waves the little petrel makes her bed; nor why, beneath the waves, "down to the dark, to the utter dark" on

"The great gray level plains of ooze,"

the "blind white sea-snakes" make their home; nor why at the north, in the fearful, far-off, frozen north, the little lemmings dwell; nor why, nor why. But as I sat there above the clouds, listening to the plaintive, trembling whistle of the little cony, and hoping his mate was not dead, and wondering why he stayed here in the barren peak, and how he must fare in the black, bitter winter, I said over to myself the lines of Kipling for an answer,—

"And God who clears the grounding berg
And steers the grinding floe,
He hears the cry of the little kit-fox
And the lemming on the snow."

NOTES AND SUGGESTIONS

CHAPTER I

TO THE TEACHER

Let me say again that the best thing any nature book can do for its readers is to take them out-of-doors; and that the best thing any nature-study teacher can do for them is to take them out-of-doors. Think of going to school to a teacher so simple, wholesome, vigorous, original, and rich in the qualities of the soul that she (how naturally we say "she"!)—that she comes to her classroom by way of the Public Garden, carrying a bird-glass in her hand! or across the fields with a rare orchid in her hand, and the freshness and sweetness of the June morning in her face and spirit! Why, I should like to be a boy again just to have such a teacher. Instead of bird-songs it is too often school gossip, instead of orchids it is clothes, instead of the open fields it is the round of the schoolroom that most teachers are absorbed in. Most teachers can add and spell much better than they can read, because they do not know the literary values and suggestions of words. Nothing would so help the run of teachers as the background, the observation and feeling, that would come from an intimate knowledge of the out-of-doors in the vicinity of their schoolrooms.

FOR THE PUPIL

Page 5

Learn first of all the joy of walking. It is enough at first to say "I am going to take a woods walk," with nothing smaller in mind to do or hear or see. Such tramping itself is one of the very best ways of meeting the wild folk, and getting acquainted with nature. Go to a variety of places—the seashore, the water-front, the upland pasture, the deep swamps, even if you take a car-ride to reach them. Then select the place nearest at hand to frequent and watch closely.

Page 6

There are many good books on the use of the camera for nature-study. Among them read: "Nature and the Camera" by Dugmore; "Home Life of Wild Birds," by Herrick.

Page 8

The clover blossom and the bumblebee: Read the intensely interesting book of Darwin's on the cross-fertilization of flowers. You will also find readable accounts in "Nature's Garden," by Mrs. Blanchan.

Page 8

In what nursery book do you find the original account of *the House that Jack Built*?

Page 9

Coccinella septempunctata: The ladybirds, or ladybugs, are named according to the number of their spots: *septempunctata* means seven-spotted. Another is called *novemnotata*, nine-spotted.

Sixty species of birds: Make your own list. Study your woods, your neighborhood, minutely day and night in order to find them all.

CHAPTER II
TO THE TEACHER

Set the students to watching and reporting this rare but very interesting phase of wild animal life. Nothing will tax their patience and ingenuity more; nor will any of their reports need so careful scrutiny and weighing, so easy is it to be mistaken.

FOR THE PUPIL

PAGE 12

"line": the end of the race; the "tape" or mark set for runners in a contest.

"set-to": a combat or fight.

mix-up: is the same half-slangy word or newspaper expression for a general fight.

PAGE 13

Paramœcium: this is one of the best known of the single-celled animals. You can get them by making an "infusion" of raw potato, a little hay, and stagnant water.

A writer in one of our magazines: The account is found in "St. Nicholas" for May, 1913.

two big slanting cellar-doors: These were in the shed of my grandfather's farmhouse, "Underwood," and covered the "bulk-head" of the cellar.

PAGE 14

The [Massachusetts] Society for the Prevention of Cruelty to Animals: has its headquarters in Boston. It does a great work for "dumb" animals, and publishes a paper called "Our Dumb Animals" that every home and school should have.

follow my leader: a game that all boys know and love, especially when a strong, daring leader takes the game in hand.

Mount Hood: is the highest peak of the Cascade Range in Oregon. The *rope* hanging down from the summit was brought up on a pack-horse or mule (I forget which) as far as Tie-up Rock, then carried to the summit by the professional guides and there fastened for the safety of those whom they take to the top during the summer.

a wild snowstorm: for a fuller description of this storm and the whole climb see the chapter in "Where Rolls the Oregon" entitled "The Butterflies of Mount Hood."

CHAPTER III

FOR THE PUPIL

"All heaven and earth are still," etc.: this is from Byron's "Childe Harold's Pilgrimage," a poem you ought to read.

Mr. William L. Finley's story of the condor appeared in the "Century Magazine." It is one of the most interesting bird stories ever written.

This is the season of flowers: among the helpful and interesting flower books for field use are "Gray's Manual," Mrs. Dana's "How to Know the Wild Flowers," and Chester A. Reed's little vest-pocket *Guide* with colored plates of the common flowers.

rain down little toads: I saw it again in the deserts of Oregon, the quick shower making millions of western spadefoot toads hop up out of the sand. As the sun came out again, presto! all were gone—into the sand out of sight.

CHAPTER IV

TO THE TEACHER

In reading this story point out the very narrow margin of life among the wild animals; that is to say, show how little a thing it often is that turns the scales, that makes for life or death. We need all our powers, and all of them developed to their very highest degree of efficiency for the race of life. Only the fittest survive, and for these the race is often under too great handicaps.

FOR THE PUPIL

PAGE 27

plumers: those who used to kill birds for their beautiful plumage.

Klamath Lake Reservation: is partly in California. It was set aside by President Roosevelt.

the coyote: is the prairie or desert wolf. He is larger than the red fox, but smaller than the gray, or timber, wolf.

PAGE 28

homesteader: one who settles upon land under the Federal home-steading laws.

CHAPTER V
TO THE TEACHER

With a map of Boston follow the course of this title—from the crowded wharf and water-front to the wide, country-like fields of Franklin Park. It is a five-cent car-ride, a good half-day's walk if you watch the wild life on the way. Map out such a course in your own city and take your pupils over it on a tramp, watching for glimpses of animal and bird life and for the sight of Nature's face—the sky, the wind, the sunshine, trees, grass, flowers, etc. Make the most of your city chance for nature-study. It is an important matter.

FOR THE PUPIL

T wharf, long one of the busiest fish wharves in the world, perhaps the busiest, is, as I write, on the point of being abandoned by the fish-dealers of Boston, who are to occupy a huge new pier at South Boston, built by the State at a cost of about a million dollars. Franklin Field is a great athletic field adjoining Franklin Park in the southern part of Boston.

Page 39

list of saints: these immortal names are carved in various places on the outer walls of the Public Library.

cranium: the head, or rather the skull.

herring gull: *Larus argentatus*, one of the largest and commonest of the harbor birds, and very much like the Western gull of Three-Arch Rocks. It is a pearl-gray and pure white creature with black on the wings. The immature birds are a brownish gray and look like an entirely different species for the first year.

Boston, Baltimore, etc.: Make a study of your city parks and the spots of green and the open spaces where the wild things may be found. Go to the Public Library and ask for the books that treat of the wild life of your city: "Wild Birds in City Parks," by Walter, will be such a book for Chicago; "Birds in the Bush," by Torrey, and "Birds of the Boston Public Garden," by Wright, for Boston.

Charles River Basin: the wide fresh-water part of Charles River just above the dam and near Beacon and Charles Streets.

Scup: another name is porgie, porgy, scuppaug.

Squid: (*Ommastrephes illecebrosus*), a cephalopod, or cuttle-fish, used for bait along the Atlantic coast.

The "cuttle-bone" in canaries' cages is taken from the genus *Sepia*.

Squeteague: pronounced skwe-tēg'; also called weakfish and sea-trout.

Scallops: are shellfish the large muscle of which is much prized for food.

These are only a few of the fish kinds brought in at T Wharf.

Grand Banks: a submarine plateau in the Atlantic, eastward from Newfoundland; noted as a fishing-ground. Its depth is thirty to sixty fathoms.

the Georges: a smaller bank lying off Cape Cod.

"We're Here": the name of the schooner in Kipling's "Captains Courageous."

Quincy Market: an old well-known market in Boston.

King's Chapel: on Tremont Street. It was begun in 1749 and is still used for worship. See "Roof and Meadow" for a fuller account of the sparrows.

rim rock: the edging of rock around the flats and plains of the sage deserts of Oregon.

Boston Common: known to every child who has read the history of our country. The "Garden" is across Charles Street from the Common.

P AGE 40

Agassiz Museum: the Museum of Comparative Zoölogy at Harvard University. It is popularly called the Agassiz Museum in honor of the great naturalist Louis Agassiz, who founded it.

See Sarah K. Bolton's "Famous Men of Science."

Arnold Arboretum: is near the western edge of Boston; one of the most celebrated gardens of trees in the world.

Through the heaven's wide pathless way: from "Il Penseroso," by Milton.

P AGE 41

Swales: wet, grassy, or even bushy, meadows.

CHAPTER VI

FOR THE PUPIL

P AGE 43

The tree-toad: (*Hyla versicolor*); he is said by country people to prophesy rain.

pennyroyal: is one of the small aromatic mints.

Wilson Flagg: one of our earliest outdoor writers. Look up his life in any American biographical dictionary.

CHAPTER VII

TO THE TEACHER

For a fuller account of this Wild Bird Reservation see the chapter in "Where Rolls the Oregon," called "Three-Arch Rocks Reservation." Bring out in your reading the point I wished to make, namely that these great reservations of State and Federal Government are not only to preserve bird and animal life, but also to preserve nature—a portion of the earth—wild and primitive and thrilling, against the constant encroachments of civilization. Interest your pupils in their own local parks, preserves, etc., and if they have farms or wood-lots, have them post them and set them aside as their personal sanctuaries for wild life.

FOR THE PUPIL

Page 51

Tillamook: the name of a town near the coast of Oregon.

at the mouth of the bay: Tillamook Bay, where the bar is only about thirty feet wide, making the passage extremely difficult and dangerous.

Three-Arch Rocks Reservation: was set aside by President Roosevelt. Credit for this and the other Oregon Reservations is largely due to Mr. William L. Finley and the Audubon Societies.

Page 53

Shag Rock: so named for the black cormorants that nest upon it, for these birds are commonly known as "shags."

the sea-lions: were of the species known as Steller's sea-lions.

reversed in shape: I mean the close hind flippers, the tapering hind end of the body, gave them an unnatural shape—reversed.

Æolus: the god of the winds.

CHAPTER VIII

TO THE TEACHER

Set the pupils to watching for evidences of mother-love among the lower creatures, where we do not think of finding it; stir them to look for unreported acts, and the hidden, less easily observed ways. Such a suggestion might be the turning of a new page for them in the book of nature.

FOR THE PUPIL

PAGE 58

Cud: the ball of grass or hay that the cow keeps bringing up from her first stomach to be chewed and swallowed, going then into the second stomach, where it is digested.

stanchions: the iron or wooden fastening about the cow's neck in the stall.

mother-principle: the instinct or unconscious impulse of all living things to reproduce their kind.

PAGE 59

spores: the name of the seed dust of the ferns.

the hunter family: these are the spiders that build no nets or webs for snaring their prey, but hunt their prey over the ground.

PAGE 60

Toadfish: See the chapter in the "Fall of the Year" called "In the Toadfish's Shoe."

PAGE 62

Surinam toads: pronounced sōō-rī-näm´.

Mother-passion... in the life of reptiles: many readers, seeing this statement in the "Atlantic Monthly," where the essay first appeared, have written me of how when they were *boys* they saw snakes swallow their young—or at least killed the old snakes with young in them! Isn't that mother-love among the reptiles? But every time the story has been about garter snakes or moccasins or some other ovoviviparous snake; that is, a snake that does not lay eggs, but keeps them within her body till they hatch, then *gives birth* to the young. I have never seen a snake swallow its young; though big snakes do *eat* little ones whenever they can get them.

CHAPTER IX

FOR THE PUPIL

Mother Carey's chickens are any of the small petrels. The little *stormy petrels* of poetry and story belong to the Old World and only wander occasionally over to our side of the Atlantic.
Page 69

petrel: pronounced *pĕt'rel*, so called in allusion, perhaps, to Saint Peter's walking on the sea.

CHAPTER X

FOR THE PUPIL

Page 76

P Ranch: is one of the Hanley system of cattle ranches, which cover a wide area almost seventy-five miles long. The buildings and tree-fences, the stockades and sheds make it one of the most picturesque I have ever seen. This story was told to me by Jack Wade, the "boss of the buckaroos." "Buckaroo" is a corruption of the Spanish *vaquero*, cowherd.

Winnemucca: find the place on the map.

Page 78

buckskin: a horse of a soft yellowish color. He got his name Peroxide Jim from the resemblance of the color of his coat to that of human hair bleached by peroxide of hydrogen.

CHAPTER XI

FOR THE PUPIL

Page 85

paper nests in trees: The common yellow-jacket hornet builds similar large round nests in bushes, and other wasps build paper nests behind walls, under the ground, in holes, etc.

Page 91

bite into something poisonous: Send to the Department of Agriculture at Washington for the little booklet on our poisonous plants. It is free.

CHAPTER XII

TO THE TEACHER

Try to bring home to the class the profoundly interesting facts of animal distribution—where they live, and how they came to live where they do. Point out the strange shifts resorted to by various creatures who live at the various extremes of height or depth or cold or heat to enable them to get a living.

PAGE 103

"*And God who clears*": these lines of Kipling I am quoting as I first found them printed. I see in his collected verse that they are somewhat changed.